S0-BJR-551

FRIDERICUS

Other Books by Frederic F. Flach

THE SECRET STRENGTH OF DEPRESSION

CHOICES: Coping Creatively with Personal Change

FRIDERICUS

A NOVEL

FREDERIC F. FLACH

LIPPINCOTT & CROWELL, PUBLISHERS
· NEW YORK ·

FIRST EDITION

Designed by Ginger Legato

Published by arrangement with Bantam Books, Inc.

U.S. Library of Congress Cataloging in Publication Data

Flach, Frederic F
    Fridericus : a novel
    I. Title.
PZ4.F581197Fr   [PS3556.L25]   813'.5'4   79-24769
ISBN-0-690-01891-6

80 81 82 83 84 10 9 8 7 6 5 4 3 2 1

To Friedrich Flacht,
Physician for the City of Worms (1623-1640)

AUTHOR'S NOTE

THIS MUCH IS FACT:

In the fall of 1966, many years after I had become a psychiatrist and had involved myself in research into the nature of depression, Dr. Oskar Diethelm, Professor Emeritus of Psychiatry at Cornell University Medical College, discovered an unusual treatise entitled "De melancholia et idiopathica et sympathica." It was published in 1620 in Basel, Switzerland, and written by Friedrich Flacht (M. Fridericus Flacht). Subsequent inquiry revealed that Fridericus was born in Worms in 1595. He studied medicine at Strasbourg in 1616 and Heidelberg in the years 1617 to 1620, and received his medical degree at Basel November 8, 1620. From 1620 to 1623 he was the physician for the city of Mulhouse. Thereafter he became the physician for the city of Worms. He is presumed to have died in or around Worms somewhere between 1639 and 1641.

The Thirty Years War began in 1618 and ended in 1648. During this time much of Central Europe and the Rhineland was laid waste.

FRIDERICUS

~1~

BY THAT SUMMER OF 1977, LIFE HAD SETTLED DOWN TO A pleasant, even pace. Predictions about the economy sounded somewhat less gloomy. My practice was busy and my patients doing well, and there had been some promising breakthroughs in my research at the clinic.

In 1972, a couple of years after my marriage to Valerie, we had purchased, at the market low, a lovely duplex apartment, high up in a tall building on a quiet, two-block-long street just north of the United Nations, facing the East River. My office was only a block and a half away and the clinic only ten blocks farther uptown. I was invariably enchanted by being able to walk out of our building past the neat rows of brick and stone town houses and the trees that lined the streets in our neighborhood. It was a small corner of New York that reminded me of one of those squares in London's West End, and it seemed untouched by the frantic pace of the city.

It was hard to believe that Jennifer was now five and that Lisa would be graduating from high school within a year. Valerie and I had been married for seven years. It was my second marriage. Caroline had died about ten years ago, and the shock and pain of that time seemed very distant.

If there was a beginning for what happened, it was on a perfectly ordinary hot day in late August. Valerie and the children were out in East Hampton, and I had a routine morning in front of me in my office.

I had three patients scheduled that morning. One of them was Sam Briggs, a physician himself, who had refused for years to admit he could ever get depressed. He had called me early one morning at home to ask me to see him right away because he couldn't get rid of an urge to kill himself. Now, six weeks later, with medication and some insight into the stresses that he had thought he could handle indefinitely without consequences, and having overcome his embarrassment about the fact that he needed any help at all, Sam was already 90 percent on the way to recovery.

At eleven I pressed the button on the telephone intercom to get the past hour's messages. "What were those calls, Bernice?"

"Two people for appointments, Dr. Pleier," said my secretary. "A wrong number . . . and Dr. Brixton, from the clinic."

"What did Brixton want?"

"A patient you saw a few months ago was admitted to the clinic last evening. A Matthew Holbein. He wants to talk with you about it."

"Matthew Holbein? What the hell!"

"I beg your pardon, Doctor?"

Matthew Holbein was the eighteen-year-old son of old friends of mine. I'd seen the boy during the Christmas holidays, three or four times. He had seemed somewhat depressed at the time—he was worried about his studies and anxious about college applications—but after a few talks he seemed to snap out of it. Mild reactive depression had been my diagnosis, and I had reassured Matthew and his family there was nothing to be concerned about. Now I could feel a wave of apprehension going through me. What had I missed?

"Sorry, Bernice. Took me by surprise, that's all. We'll have to do some rescheduling. I'm going to the clinic to see the Holbein boy now."

The clinic was a ten-story stone building on the East River, now squatting in the shadow of the modern skyscraper that had been built only a year before to replace the old general hospital. Its heaviness was accentuated rather than relieved by the small courtyard in front and the surrounding wall with its narrow pointed arches. From a distance, the door to the clinic looked so small that you could easily feel as if once you had entered you might never get out. I'd always thought that door should be changed—enlarged somehow, to give it a feeling of hope, since too many patients who had to go through it felt hopeless enough already. As a resident in training, I used to imagine that door as a means of entry to a time warp, a passage to a place where no time existed—a feeling prob- ably reinforced by my having studied Freud's theory of the unconscious as a place where events are disconnected from the restrictions of time. In the end I realized that it was probably a matter of pacing. Outside, the frenetic world of the city pressed onward, obsessed with minutes and seconds, while inside reality was suspended, often too much so, and the staff and patients alike drifted along in a world without calendars.

I went first to the staff room to get my white coat. Then I went to Dave Brixton's office.

"What's this about the Holbein boy?"

3

Dave looked up from some papers he had been shuffling through. "Came in last night, by ambulance, from a small hospital in New Hampshire. Bad shape. Probably schizophrenic. Won't talk much. From what we can piece together, he's pretty delusional."

I sat down, tired and disbelieving, in the large brown-leather chair in front of Brixton's desk.

"I saw him a few months ago."

"So I gather."

"He was slightly depressed. Worried about school and his future. But there was no evidence of anything more serious."

"That's the way these things can start. You know that, Fred." Someone else might have said it condescendingly, but Dave was simply offering some doctor-to-doctor reassurance. "We can all miss a diagnosis. Maybe it was too early to call it."

"I just don't get it." I felt a surge of annoyance at myself. "I should have ordered psychological testing."

"Would it have really made any difference?" Dave asked.

"I'm usually good at picking up more serious disturbances, even when the symptoms aren't that clear."

Dave smiled. "You can't win them all," he said.

"This one's more complicated, Dave. I've known the Holbeins and their children for years—Matthew's the oldest of three. His parents were close to Caroline and me when she was alive. We used to spend New Year's eves together, and took a couple of trips. In fact, I knew Cynthia before I met Caroline, dated her a few times. They were roommates at college."

"You *are* involved," Dave commented. Then, thoughtfully, he went on. "I'd like to go over the history with you, Fred. Then I'd like you to see Matthew and get your ideas about what we should do now."

The facts were still quite clear in my mind. "He went off to boarding school the year before last, his junior year. First time away from home. Everything seemed fine, no trouble adjusting. Then, last fall, in his senior year, he started losing weight, not eating properly. His grades, which had been quite good, went down. He withdrew from his activities. A local doctor couldn't find anything wrong with him and referred him to the school psychologist for therapy. During the Christmas holidays he was sort of morose, quite withdrawn. That's when the parents asked me to see him. As I said, he seemed to pull right out of it, went back to school in good spirits."

Dave made notes rapidly.

"I spoke with the Holbeins about three months ago, and they said everything was going along fine. That's the last I heard."

Dave picked up from there. "Just before school closed—late in May—the parents had received an urgent phone call from the headmaster. Matthew had locked himself in his room. He was yelling and screaming, and the students in the corridor could hear him banging his fists against the walls. They got the security guard to break in and found him writhing around on the floor, his arms bleeding from a dozen wounds he had inflicted on himself with a penknife. Not a suicide attempt, apparently. More like mutilation."

"Then what?"

"He was hospitalized locally. He wouldn't talk, just sat in his room, staring, terribly depressed. After a month and a half on Thorazine, without any real effect, the doctors recommended shock treatments. But the family would have none of it and arranged for him to be transferred here. He came in last night."

With a certain amount of reluctance I asked a painfully logical question. "Why didn't the family get in touch with me?"

"I'd rather not prejudice your examination," Dave said, in a serious tone. "I'll go into that after you see him."

I was annoyed. "I'd like to know now."

"Later."

Dave could be stubborn. There was no point in pushing him. "Any lab findings?"

"Carr's the resident on the case. He's done a physical. Negative. We have a report on a brain-wave test from the sanitarium in New Hampshire, and it's a little peculiar. Shows a sleep pattern when he obviously wasn't asleep—mostly dream patterns, REM. I don't know what to make of it. We'll repeat it, of course."

"CAT scan?"

"They did one. Negative."

"And your initial impression?"

"Everything points to schizophrenia."

"But no response to Thorazine. How do you explain that?"

"I can't at the moment."

"You mentioned delusions. Of what?"

"Later. After you've seen him yourself."

Standing in front of the elevators, I pulled out my key and inserted it into the safety lock. The door opened only halfway, as it always seemed to do, and I had to push it the rest of the way. Slowly the elevator lumbered upward to the sixth floor, where I repeated the procedure. At the nurses' station I picked up Matthew Holbein's chart, which told me that he had not slept since his admission and had refused any and all kinds of medication. The nurse confirmed that he had not left his room, had not eaten, and had to be catheterized in order to pass urine.

A male orderly, assigned to stay with him constantly to prevent any further self-injury, met me at the door of his room.

"Dr. Pleier's here, Matthew," he said as I entered.

"Thank you," I said quietly to the orderly. "You can leave us alone."

Matthew was sitting in a leather chair, staring into space. His hands gripping the arms of the chair were as white as the bandages on his forearms. He looked incredibly thin and haggard. His face was gaunt, his mouth frozen in a curious smile. But when he turned to look at me, I saw pure terror in his eyes.

I walked over and sat on the edge of the bed next to him. The room itself had been stripped of any movable objects, in keeping with the security efforts of the ward. The arched window, narrow and tall, that looked out onto the East River added to the room's severity and gave it the medieval quality of a monk's cell.

"Matthew?"

No answer, of course.

"Do you remember me, Matthew? I'm Dr. Pleier."

The only movement was his shallow breathing.

"I'm here to help you. But you have to tell me what's been happening."

He turned toward me and said, in a barely audible whisper. "You know."

"No, Matthew, I don't. Only if you tell me."

"You're the only one who knows." His hands

clutched the arms of his chair more tightly.

"Tell me anyway, Matthew." I reached out and touched the bandages on his right arm gently. "What happened, Matt?"

"What am I doing here?" I could hardly hear him.

"You've been sick. This is a hospital. We're here to help you get well again."

"I'm not sick."

"Maybe that's the wrong word, Matt. Forgive me. But you are certainly troubled. You look positively terrified."

"You know why," he repeated.

"Tell me anyway, even if you think I know."

He began to mumble, incoherently, and to rock back and forth. I hadn't seen a schizophrenic patient with this symptom since my medical-student days at Bellevue. Even then, it had stirred up a severe sense of personal helplessness in me.

Then, as suddenly as he had begun, he stopped rocking, and his face became contorted with rage. He began tearing the bandages off and ripping at his wounds with his fingernails. Before I could restrain him, he bent down and savagely bit the back of his left hand, drawing blood. I rushed to the buzzer on the wall, and within twenty seconds two nurses were there to hold him until he could be given a sedative.

Back in Brixton's office, I told him what had happened. "I couldn't get enough out of him to be sure of the diagnosis."

"Did he recognize you?"

"Hard to say."

Dave was silent for a minute. Then he stood up

and walked over to the large window overlooking the court-yard the patients used for recreation on sunny days. Today was overcast and the yard was empty. He turned and looked at me intently.

"Among other things, Matthew is convinced he's under the influence of some supernatural force. He thinks he's being pulled into some kind of void or black hole in time and has to use all his energy to fight off whatever this influence may be."

"What else?"

Dave hesitated and then said quietly, "He thinks you're his real father."

I was stunned and remained silent for a moment. "You got that from him?" I asked incredulously.

"No."

"Carr?"

"No. He told his parents during one of their visits to him in the other hospital. Frankly, that's why they were hesitant to call you."

"I don't get it."

"Oh, come on, Fred, you can't expect the Holbeins to recognize delusions right off and know they're creations of the patient's mind. You used to go out with Cynthia. You said that yourself. And you were all close for years. After Matthew told them that, they had a pretty bad fight, Mrs. Holbein accusing her husband of being insensitive and largely responsible for Matthew's illness, with Mr. Holbein accusing her of being unfaithful."

"That's ridiculous!"

"Look. We both know it's ridiculous. The boy's known you for years. You saw him in consultation. It's not unusual for a strong feeling about the doctor to become part of a delusion if the patient falls apart. The doctors explained that to the Holbeins. So did I, when I saw them earlier this morning. I think they understand it now."

I still felt uncomfortable.

"The question is, Fred, what do we do now?"

"What do you have in mind?"

"Shock."

I said quickly, "I couldn't disagree with you more, Dave!" I wasn't surprised by his suggestion, but I rarely recommended electric shock treatments. On the few occasions when I did, it was primarily in older people who were likely to have adverse reactions to drugs.

"I'd rather get a clearer picture of what's going on before we consider using shock," I went on. "Seems to me our biggest risk is making Matthew worse. With the right kind of care, I don't see why we can't ease him out of it over a period of time."

"I think you're a bit optimistic," Dave replied. "But I'm willing to go along, for a while anyway. Of course," he added, almost as an afterthought, "you're basically a consultant in this case, Fred. The final decision is not really yours to make."

I canceled my five o'clock appointment and asked Bernice to have the Holbeins come by to see me instead.

Cynthia Holbein, a slim, attractive woman in her early forties, sat stiffly on the yellow sofa. Her husband, Frank, dressed in the gray pin-striped Brooks Brothers suit of the Wall Street investment broker, sat in the chair next to her.

"Dr. Brixton said he was going to explain to you why we didn't call you right away, Fred," Frank said, looking slightly embarrassed.

"He did. He also said you now understand that Matthew is delusional."

Cynthia tried to restrain her anger, but couldn't. "I don't understand why you didn't realize how sick Matthew was when you saw him at Christmas."

"Cynthia," I said earnestly, "I don't understand that myself. But there was really no evidence of a serious disorder at that time. And Matthew seemed to respond to therapy beautifully."

"You know how difficult this is for us, Fred," Frank said. "Even though we've been good friends, I've never really figured out psychotherapy. Never thought it could do much good."

Frank had always thought the nicest compliment he could offer me was to say that I didn't look or act like a "shrink." Except for me, his only contact with psychiatry had been during his physical for the Navy, when a bored, middle-aged man, peering out from behind rimless glasses, asked him what he did in his spare time, and when he could not elicit an account of any hallucinations or perverse sexual practices after two minutes of effort, dismissed him and called in the next recruit.

"Have you seen Matthew?" Cynthia asked.

"This morning."

"What's wrong with him?" she asked curtly.

"I don't know yet. None of us knows. I thought if we could go back over some of the history again, it might give us a better idea."

"Is he schizophrenic?" she asked, using the term with little understanding of it.

"I don't know, Cynthia. Even if he is, that doesn't mean he can't get well."

11

Cynthia started to cry, but quickly regained her composure. "What do you want to know, Fred?"

"Everything either of you can think of. Let's start by telling me when you think he first seemed different in any way. I know you've been over this before, and you've talked with the other doctors about it, but we might stumble on some important clues you hadn't thought of then."

Frank began, hesitantly. "Matthew seemed fine until he went back to school this past fall. You know about the trouble he had with his studies and his depression at Christmas. The fact is that until we got the call from the school and went to put him in the hospital up there, we never suspected there was anything seriously wrong. We were planning to go up for graduation."

"He was hospitalized for about two months there?"

"About that," Frank replied, looking at Cynthia for verification. "Maybe a little more."

"What happened then?"

"Frankly," Cynthia said, "he wasn't getting any better. If anything, he seemed worse. When the doctors wanted to give him electric shock, I insisted he be brought here for another opinion."

"We wanted him near home, and besides, in spite of"—Frank coughed a couple of times—"the problems along the way, we wanted you involved, because you know Matthew and that might make a difference."

"You had no other clues that something was really going wrong?"

"None," Cynthia said.

Frank seemed to have an afterthought.

"There was that business of running away, back in February."

"Running away?"

Cynthia took over. "Frank got a call from the head-master one afternoon at his office. Matthew had apparently taken off, by himself. He left his ten o'clock class and didn't show up for his next one. By four thirty, the dorm proctor became worried and told the headmaster, who thought he might have run off home. But he hadn't."

"Where did he go?"

"Lord knows," said Frank. "He was gone all that night and most of the next day. They put out a police call on him. That evening he showed up back at school for dinner. He seemed slightly confused, or so we were told, and claimed he couldn't remember what he had done."

"Could there have been drugs involved?"

"Matthew? Never," said Cynthia.

"I'm pretty sure not," added Frank.

"What about childhood?" I asked, shifting ground abruptly. "Any unusual events you can recall?"

The two of them thought for a moment. "Nothing I can think of," said Frank.

"The girls are okay? Let's see—how old are they now?"

"Fifteen and twelve," said Frank. "They're fine."

"Did Matthew, growing up, seem different from the others in any way?"

"He was very normal," Cynthia insisted. "More active physically than the girls have ever been."

"Anything at all unusual?"

Frank was becoming tense and slightly annoyed, but he could add nothing.

"Anything the least bit unusual?" I pushed on. "Walking? Talking? Physical development? Starting school? Getting on with other children?"

"Nothing," Cynthia repeated.

"Wait a minute," Frank interrupted, a look of surprise on his face. "Matthew was a more imaginative child than the others. He was always making up stories, pretending to be someone else . . ."

"All children do that, Frank," Cynthia said sharply.

"No, Cynthia, this was different. Don't you recall? He had a period when he had a whole scheme worked out. Not playing Superman or Cowboys and Indians or anything like that. I haven't thought about this in years. We'd given him a set of building blocks for Christmas— no, for his birthday—"

Cynthia broke in. "He was born on Christmas Day, but we always celebrated his birthday a month later. It seemed unfair to have it on Christmas."

Frank continued, concentrating. "We'd given him these blocks. He must have been five. He'd play for hours in his room with them. He'd always build the same thing. A city, he called it. With a wall around it. And a church and some houses. And when he finished, he'd say there was a war and he'd knock it down and build it all over again, in exactly the same way. I remember that he kept up this same game for months."

"That's right. I'd forgotten about that," said Cynthia. "When I asked him about it, he said it was his city and he lived in it with his family and that there was a river nearby with boats on it. Sometimes, in a strangely serious way, he would say that we were not his real parents. I'd get annoyed and I'd make him pick up his things and play something else."

I made a note of it. "This stage passed?"

"I spoke to the pediatrician about it," Cynthia said. "I was concerned about the intensity of it. But he said to ignore it, to make Matthew play with other children more. I did. After a few months it was gone."

"He used to get so intense playing that game. That's what really bugged us," Frank added. "Like he really believed it."

"Was anything special going on at that time? Any stresses in the family?"

The Holbeins were silent, sifting through their memories. "No, nothing," Cynthia said.

"Those were good years, as a matter of fact," Frank added.

I put down my pad. The interview was nearly over. There were only bits and pieces to work with—fragments of a puzzle.

Cynthia leaned foward, hands clenched.

"Will he be all right?" she asked.

"I'm sure he will," I reassured her, concealing my own serious confusion about what was really going on.

As I often did in the summer when Valerie was in the country, I ate dinner by myself that evening, at one of the bar-restaurants that line First Avenue in the Fifties and Sixties. When I got home I turned on the ten o'clock news on television. Martin Abend was embroiled in a vehement argument with Sidney Offit over welfare budgets, when the phone rang. It was Valerie.

"I'll be coming down on the jitney lunchtime Friday," I told her.

"We've had fabulous weather," she said. "I hope it holds out for the weekend. How is everything?"

Hearing her voice was the first thing to make me feel good again since my talk with Brixton that morning. I told her about the Holbein case.

15

"Are you sure you're not his father?" she asked lightly.

"For Christ's sake, Val. I don't think that's funny."

"I'm sorry, darling. It's not like you to get so involved with a patient. You've always been able to keep a healthy distance. And no one can be right all the time, even you."

"I didn't mean to be short with you, Val. I really don't know why I'm this upset about it. Tired, I guess."

After I had hung up I felt a strong urge to pick up the phone and call Valerie back, just to hear her voice again, to feel that everything was going to be all right. I poured myself a glass of milk and watched the first half of a rerun of "The Rockford Files" before going to bed.

Friday morning I stopped by the hospital to check on Matthew's condition before taking off for the country for the weekend. There was no change. All the way out to East Hampton I had to fight off the image of him sitting in the white hospital room, peering at me with strangely vacant eyes or, earlier, telling me I was the only one who knew what was really happening to him. It haunted me, and only the sight of Valerie waiting at the jitney stop in front of the VFW hall dispelled it.

~2~

I HAD SPENT EVERY SUMMER IN EAST HAMPTON FOR NEARLY
fifteen years, while Caroline was still alive and later alone
with our small daughter. Lisa had been only six when her
mother died suddenly of a cerebral aneurysm. There were
moments afterward when I wanted to die too. But there
was Lisa, sad, confused, needing me as much as I needed
her, if not more.

My life seemed finally to make sense again two years
later when I met Valerie. I was thirty-seven. Val was ten
years younger, sensitive, sure of herself, and very pretty.
She had just published her first mystery novel. We were
married a year later.

The house in East Hampton that we had rented
for several years now was a two-story, white-clapboard
Dutch colonial on Fithian Lane. The A&P was only five
minutes' walk away, so we could easily shop for groceries,
also light bulbs and all those other things not included
with the rental fee, and push the carts all the way home
if we wanted. It was an equally short stroll for the morning
newspapers and even shorter to the local movie house.
Fithian Lane was a one-way street, leading from Main

Street and curving for no more than a quarter of a mile to end at Egypt Lane.

A right turn on Egypt Lane took you directly to the beach, another quarter mile on. First you passed some small, white, well-preserved prerevolutionary homes. Then you would go by several considerably more ornate houses, evidence of the opulence that had been steadily moving into the town for some years. Finally you would come to open fields and a broad, richly green golf course that swept down to a pond on one side and rolled forward ahead of you to the Maidstone Club, a large Edwardian mansion on the cliffs above the sea that seemed to have been there forever.

I was one of the few doctors who belonged to the club and the only psychiatrist. It was a bastion of conservatism, but that was not why I had joined. I had a few friends there. The planter's punches were good. I liked a bacon, lettuce, and tomato sandwich for lunch and a shower after spending a few hours on the beach.

Unlike many of my colleagues, I rarely took the whole month of August off. Instead, I'd come down and join Valerie for long weekends, and then stay a few extra days over Labor Day. The sand and sea were my therapy, one sure way to clear my mind and feel renewed. Lisa and Jenny and I would build sand forts and run after one another in the surf, and by the time September arrived, we'd be bright brown and hoping that the last few days would be sunny and the sea calm so we could float endlessly with the waves, unafraid, almost motionless, smelling the salt and watching the shoreline bob up and down in a gentle rhythm.

This, however, was to be our last summer there. Valerie and I had decided to seek out some simpler place.

The village had grown up. A new shopping center had replaced the plain old frame buildings behind Main Street. Expensive development homes were springing up on every inch of unused land. On weekends, the traffic through the town's center would be snarled for hours. Next year we would go elsewhere, the Massachusetts islands, perhaps, or Europe.

The first warning that this might actually be our last summer together anywhere came in the form of a five-dollar prophecy.

Each year, on the last weekend in August, the East Hampton Village Fair was held on the grounds of the Episcopal Church, next to the little cottage called Home Sweet Home. This summer Valerie had been asked to be on the fair committee, so we took a somewhat more than ordinary interest in the event. There were the usual sorts of diversions that such fairs offered: pony rides for children (we left Jenny happily waiting her turn), homemade delicacies for sale, objects of art whose interest rarely survived the impulsive purchase of them, and, of course, a raffle. This year the committee had also included a fortune-teller.

"Go ahead, Fred, have your fortune told. Don't be a drag," insisted Marsha Allenden. Marsha was a member of the committee whom neither Valerie nor I were very fond of, although the worst thing Marsha could ever say to you or about you was that in one way or another you were sabotaging a party. Twenty pounds overweight, peering out from behind gigantic white-framed sunglasses, wearing too much lipstick and too many bits and pieces of jewelry, however genuine, she had a caustic and rather gravelly voice; and no professional experience was required to detect that she had a struggle with alcohol and was not winning.

"It's not my speed," I said, starting to walk away.

Valerie took my arm. "Why don't you? Go ahead— it's only a joke."

"Why waste five dollars hearing someone tell you that you're intelligent and have a great future and that your love life is going to improve when it's good already?"

"It's for charity," Marsha put in, trying to shake a handful of guilt onto the conversation, making it sound as if to be unwilling to spend a few dollars to have your palm read was to be a traitor to village improvement.

"If it goes against your scientific mind, I'll do it," said Valerie, smiling.

"Okay. Okay." I threw up my arms. I had long since learned that the best way to settle this kind of predicament was to comply and get it over with. "But if she promises me a great trip and terrific romance I might just take her up on it," I added.

The fortune-teller or gypsy, or whatever she was, was located predictably in a small, stuffy tent with an excess of cheap scented candles. Having purchased my ticket, I pulled the flap aside and went in. To my surprise, she was a perfectly ordinary-looking young woman—quite young, in fact—and spoke without any trace of an accent, something I had assumed would be part of the act.

"Please sit down," she said, pointing to a folding metal chair in front of a card table. I noticed a large pack of cards on the table as I sat down across from her.

"Do you wish me to use the Tarot?" she asked, indicating the cards.

"As you like." She doesn't even want to look at my palm, I thought, somewhat disappointed.

There was the ritual of shuffling and having me put my hands on the pack and then cut it. She started setting the cards out in a pattern. Each card had a picture on it, some with titles along the bottom in big capital letters. Any that faced her were upside down to me, and vice versa.

"That one's not very encouraging," I said jokingly, pointing to one facing me, with a picture of a man dangling by an ankle. The title on it was THE HANGED MAN. She ignored my attempt at humor and continued to place the cards. Then she studied them carefully for a moment and began to speak.

"You're a professional man, a lawyer perhaps, or a doctor, and quite successful. You have a very nice life." Why not say that? I thought; after all, this is the East Hampton Village Fair. Most of the people here have pretty good lives, materially speaking at any rate. And it's a safe assumption that most of the men are either business executives or professionals. Score one on a fifty-fifty chance for success.

"You have had some very difficult times in your life," she went on. At forty-four, I thought, who hasn't?

"You have two children, I believe." Good guess.

"I see a second marriage, a recent one, and you and your new wife are very much in love." Her batting average was improving. Still, one out of three marriages end in divorce, and 80 percent of the divorced remarry. Or maybe Valerie had already spoken to her and that was why she suggested I do this. For a second I wondered what would have happened if I had been married only once and were struggling to decide whether to stay married, and had the added input of a mystic to help me make my choice. I never doubted for a minute that more people consult fortune-tellers than psychiatrists, and the idea had never failed to puzzle and annoy me.

At this point, she sat there silently, her hands moving over the cards.

"Thank you very much. Are we finished?"

She did not reply. Instead, I noticed that she had begun to tremble somewhat. Her eyes closed, her face grew ashen.

"Are you all right?" I asked.

"I don't know. I don't know what's happening."

If this is part of the whole performance, I thought, it's getting quite convincing. I was feeling a bit nervous myself.

Her eyes were still tightly shut. "I have a vision of tears and sadness and much fear. I see fire and many people dying and you are trying to save them and you cannot. And everything you know now will be gone. Your life as it is now will vanish. You will feel utterly hopeless, but you will emerge more genuine than you are now."

It was becoming frightening as well as convincing, and I resented it. After all, I thought, this was for charity.

She slowly opened her eyes and looked directly at me. In a hoarse whisper she said, "Your son is in terrible trouble."

"But he's not my son! I mean, I'm not his father," I stammered, startled by my confused reference to Matthew Holbein. Then, regaining control of myself, I said, "That can't be. I have no son."

"I only told you what I saw," she said, and muttered something that sounded like "I couldn't help it."

"You see these things in the cards?"

She struggled for composure. "Not exactly . . . partly . . . every card has a symbolic meaning, you know, and I'm supposed to have learned them all, but they say it takes years to really . . ." Her voice trailed off.

This confused me further, and I said rather sharply, "Well—how do you know what you think you see?"

"I don't know. I'm so sorry." She began to cry.

"It's all right," I said reassuringly, forgetting for the moment that I was the one who was getting the bad news. "But I don't understand . . ."

"Actually, I'm pretty much of a beginner—been doing it for fun at parties. This is my first fair—for money, that is. They say that concentrating on cards or someone's palm tends to release a person's psychic faculties. But so far with me it's been mostly routine. I try to pick up the good meanings, to reassure people and make them feel better. The negative meanings are supposed to be played down. Sometimes I offer warnings, but they aren't very specific—don't speculate with money, don't be careless during a trip lest there be an accident. Things like that. But this was different."

"Different?" Now she was even getting me to take the thing half seriously.

"So vivid. This kind of thing has only happened to me once or twice before . . . as if something outside me seizes my spirit and takes over, and when I close my eyes what I see has the clarity of a photograph . . . I saw you and the fire and the look of sadness on your face and a young boy calling to you, and you were unable to move in any direction, and you were so terribly alone." She reached for a tissue and wiped her eyes. "I am sorry. Please don't put too much stock in it."

"Don't worry. I won't." I rather liked her honesty, but it only served to reinforce the impression that she must have really seen the images she described, that she had not made it all up for my benefit—unless she was, in addition to being a fortune-teller, a brilliant young actress.

Valerie was waiting outside.

"What happened, darling? You look awful."

"Was that some kind of joke?" I asked, half smiling.
"What do you mean?"
I told her.
"That's ridiculous!" Valerie protested, and added, "I think that's terrible—at this kind of event especially. Put it out of your mind." She took my hand.
"Okay," I said. "Let's go find Jenny and get some ice cream."
But I could tell from the expression of concern on Val's face, the taut little line that had jumped up between her eyes, that she could not dismiss my experience that instantly herself.

There are several ways in which things start to go wrong. Sometimes it happens suddenly. Life seems perfect. So you stop looking over your shoulder for trouble, and it suddenly drops on you like a girder from a construction site thirty stories up. I remember one of my patients, a man in his late forties who had lived for years in a nice house in New Canaan, Connecticut, and had two children in the local high school and was vice-president of a large advertising agency. In less than two weeks he lost is job, discovered that his wife had been having an affair for months with his best friend, and saw his eldest son arrested for trafficking in drugs. I was called to see him in consultation in the neurological unit of the hospital after he had unsuccessfully tried to blast his head off with a .22 rifle, destroying about a third of his brain in the process.
More often, however, bad luck or misfortune begins in bits and pieces, little warning signals that are like the little gusts of wind, the first drops of rain that are omens of a cloudburst to come. Or it's the stillness that warns

you. And the crazy things that simply don't make sense.

Lying in bed that night, I could hear the voice of the fortune-teller in the darkness. "Your son is in terrible trouble." It made no sense at all. "Everything you know now will be gone." I could feel a chill run through me. I already knew what that was like; I knew the anguish involved in having to start all over, from the beginning, to pick up the pieces and rebuild. I didn't want to go through it again.

Caroline had been on her way to a meeting of the parents' guild at Lisa's school when it happened. Crossing Third Avenue, she had barely reached the far curb when she suddenly slumped to the ground in a coma. She died before reaching the hospital, of a cerebral aneurysm. Less than three months later, my father was killed in an automobile accident. I could still hear the distant, professional—though not uncompassionate—words of the New Jersey state trooper telling me there had been an accident. A large chemical truck had run through a stop sign and smashed into my father's old Studebaker, which he had refused ever to part with. The car was a shambles and he had been killed. "Instantly," the patrolman said. "He couldn't have suffered." He truly wanted to help me, but I could only feel myself in the little car, the mass of steel crashing down on me and the impact and terror and blazing pain, and then nothing.

I lost myself in my work—as much as I could. There were times when I would sit with patients and listen to them describe their anguish and confusion and think I couldn't get through the next hour and wonder where they found their strength to go on. I didn't want to go anywhere or do anything, except be with Lisa. Friends were always trying to pair me off with someone or other, but it was nearly two years before I had any interest in even faintly cooperating with them.

And then I met Valerie.

Valerie was an only child. Her parents had been killed in a plane crash when she was eleven, and she had been brought up after that by her mother's sister, Margaret Gregory, and Margaret's husband, Alfred. Valerie understood at once what Lisa must have gone through. And as I came to know her better, I found something very special between us that I had never known, not even with Caroline—a closeness, a quiet respect for each other's feelings, a giving. She would listen to me talk about my research and I would listen to her working out a new idea for one of her mystery stories and we would hold hands walking on the street, and when we would say good-bye, even for a few hours, it had much of the romance of the first good-byes, when we knew that we were in love. She did have a mind of her own, to be sure, and an atrocious temper at times, but she never struck out to hurt.

There is no way, I thought lying in the dark, that I am going to lose this.

I reached over and rested my hand on hers—gently, so as not to wake her.

~3~

back to New York. I was scheduled to see Matthew later that day, after making rounds at the clinic, on the ward where my research studies of depression were being carried out. We usually had six or seven patients under study at any one time, each one receiving carefully measured diets to control the intake of the minerals and other substances which were the focus of our investigations. The dietitian, two student nurses, a resident psychiatrist, and Miss O'Connell, the chief nurse, were sitting with me in the nurses' station of the unit, reviewing the week's work. There were some exciting results tending to confirm the connection between calcium retention in the body and recovery from depression. Miss O'Connell raised a problem about patient care.

"It's the attitude of the doctors doing psychotherapy with these patients," she said. "As soon as the patients are assigned to the research unit, you'd think they'd been removed from the hospital. Take Mrs. Athens, for example. Her doctor had been seeing her four times a week, for an hour each visit. He really didn't want her brought down

27

here. For the last four weeks he's been coming by to see her twice a week and staying only about fifteen minutes."

I smiled. It was a familiar syndrome. I knew that as soon as the patient was returned to an exclusively psychiatric unit, her therapist's interest would be mysteriously reactivated. Many doctors have a hard time thinking of patients in a whole way, preferring to divide them neatly into entirely psychological, physical, or environmental compartments.

I glanced at the clock on the station wall. It was five of twelve. "What's the noon conference today?"

Miss O'Connell peered through her glasses at the list pinned to her bulletin board.

" 'The Evolution of Parapsychology,' " she read aloud.

"I can skip that one," said Bob Perkins, the resident, chuckling.

"I could too," I said. "But I suppose I'll have to go. I doubt that they'll get much of a showing, and Dr. Brixton counts on some of us senior people to be there for moral support. Who's the lecturer?"

"A Dr. Adam Rheinhart," Miss O'Connell said. "From California."

"Where else?" commented Bob.

Miss O'Connell said quickly, "Oh, I saw him on TV last week. He was very interesting."

I immediately pictured a wild-haired showman with way-out ideas.

To my surprise, the auditorium was nearly half filled. There were forty or fifty people—nurses, medical students, social workers, a few psychiatric residents. Dave Brixton was nowhere in sight. I was five minutes late and Rheinhart had already begun.

Rheinhart, far from being a wild-haired showman, was a serene-looking man with thick gray hair, a few years older than myself, impeccably dressed in a dark blue suit. He was too tall for the podium and had to hunch over it to see his notes.

"Scientific research regarding whether the human personality survives physical death has been going on for nearly a century," Rheinhart was saying. "And this trend can generally be divided into several phases. The earliest extends from the late nineteenth century to the nineteen thirties, during which serious investigators collected and analyzed spontaneous experiences of persons claiming to have seen apparitions of the dead or to have communicated in some way with discarnate spirits."

Rheinhart had correctly assessed his audience. He knew he would encounter some curiosity but considerable skepticism. He was using the documented, orderly approach that would add greater credence to his remarks.

"Alfred Russel Wallace, who, as you may know, developed independently of Darwin the theory of evolution, was an ardent spiritualist. So were several Nobel Prize winners, like J. J. Thomson and Henri Bergson. And William James. The Society for Psychical Research was founded in London by men of such caliber in 1882. It was a group which insisted on a highly systematic inquiry into so-called supernatural phenomena."

He raised his eyes to look at the technician in charge of the lights and slides. "Let me have the first slide, please."

The room darkened slightly.

"Here you see some of the earliest studies done. For example, in this one seventeen thousand randomly selected informants were questioned about hallucinatory experiences—seeing, hearing, touching—involving apparitions of the dead. Ten percent reported having had such experiences, and most of these were visual."

He tapped his pointer against the screen, calling for the next slide. It was a picture of a woman.

"This is Mrs. Leonore Piper, one of the most important American mediums," he said, "discovered by William James. Careful investigations could show no trickery or deception in Mrs. Piper's seeming ability to communicate with the dead. Typically, during a seance, a personality other than that of the medium seems to emerge, a trance personality known as the control, who acts as the intermediary with the deceased."

Rheinhart showed a few more slides and asked for the lights.

"By the end of this period of investigation, opinion remained seriously divided as to whether the unusual observations gathered confirmed life after death or whether visions and communication experiences alike only reflected a super-extrasensory ability on the part of the subject or the medium. One theory proposed that the medium, for example, could elicit, subconsciously, information about the deceased not only from people in the room but even from others at some distance from the seance."

He paused. "Any questions?"

Several hands went up. Halfway through the answer to the first query, Dave Brixton hurriedly entered the auditorium, looked around, spotted me, and took a seat next to mine. He was obviously disturbed.

"You've got some nerve," I whispered jokingly, "telling us to come to this lecture and then showing up late."

He didn't laugh.

"We've got a tough one, Fred." He was breathing heavily. "Matthew Holbein . . . he's gone."

I stiffened. "What are you talking about?"

"Gone. Vanished. Somehow he got out."

"I thought he was still on constant . . . someone with him all the time."

"The attendant left the room for a couple of minutes . . . the boy seemed okay . . . when he came back, Matthew was gone."

"Where?"

"I don't know yet."

"A hell of a constant! Constant means constant!" I was furious.

"The nursing supervisor and Carr are checking it out now. We'll find him. He's got to be in the building somewhere."

"He'd better be."

Rheinhart was saying something about time for one more question.

"We'd better go and check it out ourselves," I said, making a move to get up. Brixton put his hand on my arm, pressing me down.

"No point. They'll find him. We can look into it right after the conference."

"The next period of investigations," Rheinhart went on, "lasted about thirty years, until 1960." I struggled to refocus my attention.

"Here the investigators concentrated heavily on the issue of extrasensory perception, ESP. You may be familiar with some of the names associated with such studies—especially J. B. Rhine, who coined the term and pioneered the studies with his wife, Louisa. They were both biologists. The majority of the studies dealt with the theoretical ability of some persons to acquire information from the material world or from each other over various distances, independently of ordinary bodily perceptions. Playing cards, drawings, dice, and so forth were used as subject matter.

"But other researchers—for instance, Hereward Carrington and Hornell Hart—have continued to probe the question of life after death. In my present context, I think Hart's ideas deserve special mention. He found a significant resemblance between the characteristics of apparitions of people still very much alive and those of people who had died. In other words, the way in which you might have a vision of someone living but not in contact with you is quite similar to the way in which those who claim to have seen the dead experience it."

When he proceeded to discuss Gardner Murphy's theory that suggested the dead might encounter each other and discover shared interests and that this could be conveyed through a medium as information in no way obtainable while either party was still alive, I found myself giving up the effort to follow his logic. I was persistently distracted by thoughts of Matthew Holbein. Rheinhart's voice seemed hypnotic—steady and even. The word "doppelgänger" drifted by. He again asked for the lights to be dimmed and began to present studies of deathbed visions.

"An analysis of six hundred and forty questionnaires confirmed the observation that when dying persons have hallucinations they"—he read from the slide—"'predominantly hallucinate phantoms representing dead persons, who often claim to aid the patient's transition into post-mortem existence.'

"Closely related to these phenomena are the reports of people who survive after actually being pronounced dead, of having seen their physical bodies as if from another position in space."

Lights on.

I blinked and, looking at my watch, realized that we had only fifteen minutes more to go. For Christ's sake, I thought, hurry up.

Rheinhart devoted the rest of his lecture to the subject of reincarnation.

"Although it is certainly not evidence for reincarnation," he said, "it is an interesting and frequent occurrence that many subjects claiming reincarnation show personality traits, skills, and abilities that are not observably derived either from childhood experiences or from genetic sources."

There was a final, brief question-and-answer period and it was over. Dave and I would have to speak to Rheinhart, but we could get away quickly. By now, they should have found Matthew, and we'd have the facts and be ready to hand out the necessary reprimands.

Dave introduced me to Rheinhart.

"Pleier. Yes. I'm familiar with your work. Depression, isn't it?"

"That's correct, Dr. Rheinhart. I enjoyed your lecture a good deal." I hoped I sounded reasonably convincing. "Of course, I'm sure you understand I'd be a bit skeptical of your material."

"Naturally. The scientific mind, at least in the old-fashioned sense of the word 'science.' Mathematical verification and duplication. Of course you'd be doubtful." He paused. "But—you've never had an experience you could call extrasensory?"

I considered bringing up the incident with the fortune-teller at the fair in a mildly humorous way, but thought better of it. "I suppose I do get hunches. I certainly use intuition in therapy. But I'd hardly call that supernatural."

"What we look on as mysterious today may be accepted fact tomorrow, Dr. Pleier."

"Perhaps," I replied. I rather liked the man. I felt he was sincere and well informed. But we were poles apart, and besides, Dave and I had the problem of Matthew tugging at us.

Dave took care of our getaway. "You'll have to excuse us, Adam—we've got an emergency going. The residents will keep you busy, I'm sure. I'll see you later." Then he said to me, "Meet me in my office in ten minutes. I'm going to the floor to find out if everything is all right."

I waited for him nearly half an hour, going over and over in my mind the details of Matthew's case. By the time Dave came, I was shaking inside.

"They can't find him," he stated.

"What do you mean they can't find him?"

"Just what I said! He's vanished."

"How can that happen?" I'd always regarded the clinic's security system as tight as Sing Sing's.

"Someone must have left the door to the unit ajar, not pulled it tight behind them entering or leaving. How he'd know enough to try the door I can't figure, but he somehow slipped through."

"And the elevators? They have locks too."

"I don't know. A matter of timing again. Someone must have stopped at the sixth floor at that moment and, thinking Matthew had a pass to leave on his own to some activity, never questioned him."

"But he can't get out of the main door without being stopped."

"He didn't go near the main door. I've checked that out already."

"Where did he go, then?"

"We think he went out into the garden."

"But there's no way out of there."

"Not unless you climb the wall, all six feet of it, and go over."

"Into the river?"

"That's what it looks like."

"Christ."

I remembered. It had happened back in '58. A patient had gone over the wall, into the East River—had swum ashore and taken off. He was finally picked up halfway across the country. But he had been a large, strong man in his mid-twenties, a former varsity football player. Matthew could never have survived the currents in his emaciated condition. I felt like crying.

"He'll never make it," I said.

When Dave mentioned the possibility that, if Matthew had drowned, the body would no doubt show up in a few days, I wanted to shout at him. But I didn't. If you run a large clinical service, as Dave did, tragedy becomes an everyday affair and you have to learn to be dispassionate in the face of it. It didn't mean he did not care. In Dave's case, it meant that he had cared so much and for so long he could not afford to feel.

That evening, Valerie and I went out to dinner with friends. I could barely concentrate on the conversation, haunted by the feeling that what had happened to Matthew was no one's fault but my own. When the bill came, I tried to add it up, but my eyes couldn't focus on it. I asked Val to do it for me.

During the next week, no body appeared. The police were alerted, of course, but no trace of Matthew could be found. His father came to the clinic without Cynthia, who refused to see us. Frank was stricken, but strangely accepting.

"Maybe it's for the best, better than a life of madness," he said sadly. "Or maybe he's gone somewhere and will still turn up."

I could add nothing. I could only grasp his hand tightly as we said good-bye.

What I did not know and could not possibly have known then was that something—or someone, if you want to personalize fate—had started to work on the structure of my own life with an acetylene torch.

~ 4 ~

I WAS GOING TO BASEL, AND VALERIE WAS FURIOUS. SHE HAD the kind of temper that easily exploded and could just as quickly vanish. I had learned, living with her, that more often than not the flash of rage didn't mean she was really angry with me even when I was the obvious target. It was an automatic response to hide hurt or disappointment. To respond in kind could lead to a serious battle, with a dozen irrelevant issues thrown in for good measure. To ignore it could do the same.

I was in the bedroom, trying to decide just what to pack for the trip.

"Why are you taking the large suitcase?" she asked in a tone that made me feel for an instant like a four-teen-year-old boy struggling to put his things together to go to camp. "Why not just take the small canvas one?"

The vision of a small ashtray given me by a patient some years ago jumped into my head. On it was written, "The world belongs to the optimist who keeps cool."

Calmly I said, "Because I don't know what to take with me. It might be warmer there than expected for September. And I don't know how formal the whole thing will be."

Valerie walked across the room and looked out the window toward the East River, turning her back to me. "You never told me you were going this week. We just got back from the country."

"I certainly did. When I first got the invitation."

"That was months ago. You should have reminded me."

I walked over to her and tried to put my arms around her. She tightened and pulled away. "Look, Val. The last thing I want to do myself is go to Europe or anywhere right now . . . not until the Holbein boy turns up."

Her expression changed from annoyance to concern. She put her arms around my neck and pressed her head on my shoulder. "I'm sorry. It's just that I value our time together so much. I hate to be away from you."

"It's only six days."

"I know. But that's six days on top of being apart on and off all summer."

"Next year we'll plan a different kind of summer."

She walked over to the small desk next to the bed and sat down. "Maybe it's just as well you are going. I've been worried about you all week. I just don't understand why you're so obsessed with Matthew Holbein."

"You think I know why?" I replied, impatiently. "I'd give my right arm to know why."

"Promise me something, Fred."

"What?"

"That you'll go to see Mort Stein when you get back." Stein had been my analyst twenty years earlier, and later he had helped me get through the awful months after Caroline's death.

"I hardly think that's necessary, Val."

"Please, Fred. Promise me."

"All right. If it will make you feel better."

She pulled out a small memo pad from the desk drawer. "What's the name of the hotel you're staying at?"

"The Three Kings."

"In Basel?"

"Right." I went on packing. The tension had lifted. Green blazer. Blue suit. Gray slacks, two pairs, light and heavy.

I had been invited to give a lecture on my concepts and research on depression at an International Symposium on Depression. The invitation had come from Professor Heimwich at Basel, and I was incredibly pleased. For years the work I had done had received considerably more attention in Europe than in America, partly because in the early years the thinking of American psychiatry was still dominated by Freudian theory, and later because my own view of depression did not coincide with some of the more popular biochemical theories in the United States.

Ironically, Freudianism had never really taken hold in Europe, and, lacking in the kind of money American foundations and government sources could put into biological investigations, the Europeans had less of a vested interest in some particular theory to which their lives and fortunes had been dedicated. If you have a new idea and want it to be accepted, physicist Max Planck once said, wait until your colleagues retire or pass on and then present it to a new and hence less biased generation. He might have added, present it in another culture, too.

The best plane connection for me was to fly by way of Paris, so that by the time I arrived at the Basel-Mulhouse airport I was exhausted. I had left New York at six in the evening, and although it was now nearly noon in Switzerland I was still operating on a biological clock that indicated somewhere around seven in the morning. So I headed for the hotel, took a warm bath, collapsed into a deep sleep, and woke up just in time for dinner. It was the phone buzzing that roused me.

"Dr. Pleier?"

"Yes."

"Ralinsky here. Have you had a good rest?"

"Thank you." I still felt slightly incoherent.

"I thought you might like to join us for dinner."

Ralinsky. Of course. California. Stanford. Antidepressant drugs. Fine.

"Meet us in the lobby in about half an hour?"

"Fine." The urge to roll over and go back to sleep was overwhelming, best dispelled by hurriedly throwing feet on the floor, standing up, and stretching emphatically.

We ate dinner on the terrace of the hotel. It was a mild evening, still early, still light enough to see the Rhine flowing vigorously by and the old stone bridge that arched its way across from the old city, where we were located, to the north city on the other side. Every few minutes a green trolley would cross it, looking like a Marklin toy train. A large motor barge, chugging away rhythmically, moved past. It was flying a Dutch flag and on its stern was painted ROTTERDAM. Sitting on deck chairs, a woman and a twelve- or thirteen-year-old girl waved to us, and I felt a sentimental stirring, thinking of them coming all the way down the river from Holland and the excitement of suddenly passing through the center of the city and knowing that their journey was nearly completed. I mentioned my feeling to Ralinsky and the others.

"*Up* the Rhine, Friedrich," said Ralinsky. "The

Rhine flows down from its source to empty into the North Sea." I was still so tired I only now suddenly remembered that to look at a map or globe and study the course of rivers can give you quite a false sense of what is up and what is down. "Gravity is what makes rivers flow," Ralinsky went on kindly, with the faintest hint of humor, "so from the mountains of Switzerland to the lowlands of Holland the direction is down. Somehow, one does assume automatically that it should be the other way."

Ralinsky was American enough to call me by my first name, cordially, although I did not know him that well, but still European enough to call me Friedrich.

There were four of us in all. Ralinsky and I had been joined by Professor Heimwich and one of his associates, Antoine Courrailt from Paris.

Between the main course—a delicious tournedos—and dessert, we talked about the conference.

"I'm beginning to get intrigued by your theories about depression," Ralinsky said, "especially the part that emphasizes the normality of the depressed mood after serious stress and focuses on the lack of biological resilience as the real disorder."

Heimwich took a turn: "What you are implying, I assume, is that the real illness is an adaptional one, but that there is an illness there. You haven't gone so far as to say that all depression is normal and that we have to suffer through it, even at the risk of suicide and hospitalization, for some vague purpose. Like . . . what is the name of that American who keeps writing about the idea that there isn't any such thing as mental illness?"

"Szasz."

"Yes, Szasz. You haven't gone that far out on a limb, have you?" Heimwich knew the answer to his question already. If he hadn't, I would never have received the invitation. The question was a formality, a polite way to get me to talk more.

"Of course not. It's a matter of focus. If you look at the depression too closely, you miss the sequence of events—loss, disruption, depression, reintegration, renewal—that has to happen physically as well as psychologically. So that when you give an antidepressant, you're not really curing depression, but stimulating the recovery mechanisms that—for whatever reasons—have stalled and left the person stuck in the depressed mood."

"What about shock treatment?" Heimwich asked.

I thought of Matthew's disappearance. Maybe I was wrong to have opposed Brixton's giving Matthew shock. Maybe he would have responded well and then we could have reached him. Heimwich was waiting for my answer. "I don't know," I said slowly. "I'm re-evaluating some new data on shock." I was relieved to be interrupted by the waiter, who began to serve us large strawberries with whipped cream and an assortment of small crisp cookies.

"No coffee for me," said Courrailt. "The conference begins tomorrow morning at nine. I think I'll be off to bed."

"Have you been to Basel before?" asked Heimwich, as we were saying good night.

"No," I replied.

"I think you will find it a most interesting city. There will be time to visit," he assured me. "You must go to the museum of art, and of course the old city. The cathedral is only a few minutes' walk from here. And so is Petersplatz and Petersgasse. The old university was right there," he added, pointing toward the row of old houses that stretched along the riverbank on the other side of the hotel.

"Oh, Dr. Pleier. One more thing," Heimwich said.

42

"I have something interesting to show you. A surprise. Later in the week. At my office. I think it will please you."

"What is that?"

"I'd rather you find out when I give it to you." His gray eyes seemed mischievous as he looked at me, smiling in that tight way that betrayed the Swiss reluctance to show too much emotion. "Good night."

The conference itself was a smashing success, if you can consider "smashing" applicable to a group of conservatively dressed, middle-aged physicians and scientists, reading a series of papers in a special monotone that seems to suit such occasions, before an audience of a hundred or so other conservatively dressed colleagues who were permitted to ask questions for a few moments after the completion of each presentation. Every now and then the lights would be turned off and the room would be dimly lit by the slide lantern and the charts and graphs projected on a screen. Since each participant spoke in his or her own language, everyone had a set of headphones that allowed instant translation into his own language. The information itself was really not new—except for one paper that involved some original investigations into the pharmacologic action of a new set of antidepressants. But the real pleasure of the meetings was in hearing people whom you have known only in print talk about their work and the experiences they have had.

Most of the time I made a conscious effort not to think about Matthew Holbein. I did call Dave Brixton once, to find out what was going on. The boy was still missing. And one evening, over drinks, I shared my concern with Ralinsky, who tried to reassure me by reminding me that it was highly likely that all diseases such as Matthew's originated in unknown biochemical abnormalities and by suggesting that if I would concentrate wholly on my research and not waste my time doing psychotherapy I wouldn't get so hopelessly entangled with the problems of my patients.

After lunch on Thursday, the last day of the meetings, I went to Heimwich's office.

It was a large room, lined with bookcases and with a massive desk stretching in front of windows that looked out over a garden. In front of the desk were two large brown-leather chairs. Heimwich waved me into one and he sat down in the other, leaning forward as he spoke.

"Pleier. Is that a German name?" He leaned forward as he spoke.

"I suppose so. I've never traced the family. They were Huguenots, I think, perhaps from the Strasbourg area, who fled persecution into Switzerland and Germany. I know that my great-grandfather was born in Hechingen, near Tübingen, but that's all."

"Interesting. There is a small village named Pleier here in Switzerland. In Zurich canton, near Shaffhausen. Perhaps your family originated near there."

"I don't know, really." I'd always thought the American passion of searching out ancestors and building family trees somewhat suspect. It could be so easily sidetracked into an effort to locate noble origins which, more often than not, could end up in fictionalizing the past.

"As I said, I have something quite interesting to show you."

He stood up, walked to his desk, and picked up a folder which he handed to me.

I opened it, glanced in—and stared. "This is incredible," I whispered.

"Yes, indeed."

Heimwich had given me an old manuscript, marvelously preserved, no more than half an inch thick, about five inches across and eight or nine down, and coverless so that one could read the title page at once.

DISPVTATIO
DE MELANCHOLIA
ET IDIOPATHICA
ET SYMPATHICA

Below this title, in equally bold type, was the author's name, **M. FRIDERICUS PLEIERT,** and, below that, *Vormatiensis.*

It was dated MDCXX and published in Basel.

"This is incredible," I repeated. "That's 1620—just over three hundred and fifty years ago. Where did you find this?"

"One of my associates on the faculty here has a special interest in medical history. He has been studying the old records of the University of Basel, and he came across this document in the archives."

"I don't know what to say." I leafed through the pages. The dissertation was written in Latin. I could pick out a word here and there, straining my long-lost vocabulary.

"Do you have any idea what's in it?" I asked.

"None. We have not bothered to have it translated. There are many old writings, and this one did not happen to be of more than passing interest to Professor Steubens. But it is yours. We have another copy in the archives. You may keep this one."

"It is quite a coincidence. Same name. Same subject

matter. All we need now is for old Fridericus to have the same concepts of depression that I have."

"I doubt it. Many different forms of mental disease were included in the broad category melancholia in the seventeenth century. And the theory of vapors of Galen was still commonly held. Although Paracelsus had already had quite an influence, introducing the use of pharmaceuticals to treat illness."

"Safe to say it won't be Freudian."

"Quite."

"Pleiert may be a very common name, of course."

"Not really. It is actually rather unusual, here as well as in Germany."

"Was the subject a popular one in those days, psychiatry, I mean?" I asked.

"Again, no. Professor Steubens tells me that it was a rather unusual subject to choose for a dissertation. You must remember that in that period of history there were only three major professors here in Basel. The student of medicine was like an apprentice, and his work was largely tutorial. And there were perhaps no more than a dozen students at any one time. So it is unusual."

I was tempted to make a joke about reincarnation, that I was surely Fridericus returned to continue my work, but somehow I felt that the conservative Heimwich would not appreciate the humor of it.

"You can, if you wish, use our library and archives, to discover more about Pleiert and his work."

I thanked him and said that I had already planned to return home right after the conference. Actually, the prospect of digging in dusty archives for a few shreds of information about a seventeenth-century doctor whose name resembled my own was not that appealing.

46

"The name is really not the same," I said. "There's a *t* at the end of Pleier."

"True. That may be Latinized. Or perhaps a variation."

"And *Vormatiensis*? Is that 'coming from Worms'?"

"Yes. Either he originated from Worms or lived there at some point prior to his coming to Basel."

"Interesting." The initial sense of amazement that I felt when I first glanced at the manuscript had evaporated. A good story to tell Valerie, who would appreciate it. It might be amusing to have the cover Xeroxed and frame it and hang it in my office to catch a few eyes and astonish a few colleagues.

"I can't thank you enough."

Looking back now, seeing myself stand up and shake Professor Heimwich's hand, remembering what I said to him, those parting words seem grimly ironic, like the automatic etiquette that prompts one to express gratitude to a kindly face who has just informed you that the bank has foreclosed on your home or that the firm you have worked for for twenty years no longer requires your services.

~5~

ON A MONDAY IN OCTOBER, I KEPT MY PROMISE TO VALERIE and went to see Mort Stein. Morton Stein was now in his seventies. He was short, comfortably encased in Harris tweed, and had undisciplined gray hair. A perpetual cigarette which he never seemed to inhale dangled from his lips. Morton had been one of the leading figures in Freudian psychoanalysis in the 1940s and 1950s. Like so many creative personalities, he had continued to move forward in his thinking, with a restlessness and vision that had left many of his followers scrambling around behind, trying to find their own security by making dogma out of his flashes of intuitive genius, many of which he himself had long since reconsidered and redefined. He was a rare combination of warmth and brilliance and had somehow escaped the sickly egotism which, like dry rot, had attacked so many other colleagues who had won recognition for their achievements. Moreover, Morton talked. He was no wall of silence. He had opinions. He could admit being wrong. He was excited by knowing that he did not know.

As a young doctor, as part of my training, I had spent nearly four hours a week for four years lying on his couch, listening to the burning logs crackling in the fireplace, searching for understanding, and drawn on by the enormous promise that the atmosphere of analysis engendered.

"Don't idealize me," he would say. It was hard not to.

When I chose to engage in biological research and abandoned plans to go to a psychoanalytic institute, he commented only once, "Marvelous," dispelling any guilt I might have had in not following directly in his footsteps.

And when the regular sessions ended, we deliberately planned for me to revisit him from time to time to talk things over, to relieve some of the strains that he assured me I would encounter in the life of a psychiatrist. And then there was his great help when I had lost both Caroline and my father. Although I had rarely seen him outside of his office, except to say hello at a professional meeting or the University Club, Morton Stein was truly a friend.

And he was keenly interested in dreams. The fact that I hardly dreamed at all—or never recalled those dreams I had—had made me feel that I was a disappointment to him as a patient. "We can get where we have to go without them," he would say, reassuringly. But his writings, concentrating as they did on the importance of dream life in analysis, and with which I was quite familiar, watered down his reassurance in my mind.

Nonetheless, in a definitely accommodating effort, my dreaming would become especially active during the two or three days before our infrequent sessions.

"How was your trip to Basel last week?" Morton asked.

"Excellent. I really enjoyed it."

"And things with Valerie?"

"Couldn't be better."

"What made you decide to come and see me now?"

"It was Valerie's idea, frankly."

"Oh."

From the corner of my eye I caught a glimpse of his long black-leather sofa that stretched along the wall.

I hadn't stretched out on it for years, not since our regular analysis had ended. In most of our later visits I had sat in a chair, face to face with him. Today I felt a curious, fleeting urge to go over and lie down on the sofa.

"Well?" That was his invitation to me to open up and tell him whatever might be concerning me.

"I've had a dream," I said.

Morton smiled.

"Last night, in fact. I slept badly, kept waking up and going back to sleep every half hour or so. But the thread of the story kept on and I'd pick it up where I left off. Funny, it was a dream I recall having a number of times, when I was in therapy with you and before I married Valerie."

"The houses?" Morton asked. Early on I had been amazed at his ability to recall details such as this, but after years of practice myself I realized that a psychiatrist can develop a highly selective memory that is activated by the presence of his patient. If you had asked Morton yesterday what dreams I had had, I doubt that he could have remembered without checking his notes. But with me there, sitting in the room, and with his sensitive abilities tuned in, it all came back to him.

"Right. The one with the two houses. I felt I had to find the special room in the second house, the one that was familiar and safe. As usual, I was wandering across sand dunes, like the beach, at night. I found the first house, large, dark, frightening, lonely. Then I was outside again, searching for the second."

"Pretty much the same," Morton commented. "Go on."

"I could smell the sea air. There were bushes and brambles blocking my way. I came to a small rise. The water was straight ahead. But this time, instead of being the sea, it was quite clearly a broad river. The second, smaller house stood near the edge of it. I went in, and upstairs into the room. It looked out over the river. It was warm, cozy, filled with furniture, books, and things that . . . told me I was home again."

Morton spoke. "This part is quite similar, except for the river, of course. If I recall correctly, you had this dream often but without finding the second house and the room in it, until you met Valerie. And then you did. As if there were a completion in your relationship with her."

"That's right. But last night it didn't end there." I could feel a sharp and sudden change in my mood. I really hadn't thought about the dream again after getting up that morning, but now, telling Morton Stein about it, the full fury of the fear and loneliness in it swept back over me.

"What else?"

"As I stood there, in the room, the house seemed to explode in flames. I felt paralyzed, unable to move. I wanted to shout, but I felt too weak. I could hear other explosions too, in the distance. The heat and the noise of the flames was so real. Then I woke up."

"What do you think this twist at the end means?"
"I don't know."

"But you do, somewhere."

Silence. Then I told him what the fortune-teller had predicted at the fair. The nonsense about the fire and my "son" in trouble. How idiotic I had felt, identifying her remark with Matthew Holbein's plight. I gave him a brief report on Matt's case.

He listened intently, gave me one of his familiar penetrating looks, and said, "Anything else, Fred?"

Almost embarrassed, I told him about the Basel document.

"Very likely an ancestor of yours. Why wouldn't he have a type of mind that you've inherited?" He lit a cigarette. "But I'm wondering why you would be more suggestible than usual, unconsciously of course. These kinds of things would not normally reach you. The Holbein case is something else. Quite threatening to your self-confidence, I'm sure. And you haven't made the obvious connection."

"Which is?"

"Caroline was pregnant when she died. You told me the two of you had hoped for a boy."

It was as if Stein had plunged his fist into me, just below the center of my rib cage. My eyes filled up. "My God, Morton. How could I have missed that?"

"It's quite understandable," he replied gently. He waited a moment as I regained composure and then added, "In the absence of other data, we must assume that the problem of Matthew Holbein touched the grief you felt when you lost not only Caroline, but the unborn child as well . . ." He paused again. "As for the conflagration at the end of the dream . . . we can consider it a kind of existential experience. You know, when things are going well . . . really well . . . as they have been for you the past few years, there is often that lingering fear of something going wrong."

I felt vastly relieved. "Well, I'm glad you don't think it's an omen of some sort," I said, smiling.

"Tell me more about your work," Morton said.

I did. And, as I was leaving, he smiled and said, "Thanks for the dream, Fred."

I found it difficult to fall asleep that night. And when I did, I kept waking up again and again. The Sony clock on the dresser, its digits barely visible in the darkness, said it was three thirty-two.

I finally did sink into a sound sleep—and began to dream.

I was on a train. Amtrak. I knew it had come from Washington, D.C. But I was sitting in a compartment such as those one sees in European trains. The door opened and the conductor asked for my ticket.

"I don't have one. I'm sorry. How much is it to Cologne?" I asked. What the hell was I going to Cologne for?

"Eight fifty," he replied. "But you will have to change at Andreas."

I gave him ten dollars, took the change, and leaned back looking out the window. It was raining, and the rain beat against the windows with a vague hint of distant lights whirling by.

Suddenly, I was standing on a station platform. The train had gone. The rain had settled to a drizzle. A chauffeur in black uniform walked toward me.

"Dr. Pleier?"

"Yes."

"I'm the driver. Mrs. Gregory sent me to pick you up."

Aunt Margaret's chauffeur led me down a long stairway and across the parking lot to a large black limousine—an old La Salle. He opened the rear door and closed it after me. We drove for a few minutes, or so it seemed, along a country road, slowly, evenly, until we came to a large gate with iron grills, the kind you see nowadays standing alone, in isolation, crumbling a little but still stalwart testimonials to the wealth they guarded half a century ago. We moved along a winding driveway edged with elms, finally reaching the front door of a large manor house which in no way resembled the Gregorys' New England colonial.

Valerie was standing in the doorway. I wanted to embrace her and tell her I loved her but I could not move. I could not understand what she was doing there, or what I was doing there either, for that matter.

The Sony said five twelve.

I was in a small bedroom toward the back of the upstairs hallway. It seemed quite cramped. There was no window and I wondered if someone had made a mistake. Hearing a shuffle outside the door, I opened it. My father was softly walking along the hall. It seemed natural for him to be there. I called out to him but he did not seem to hear me. I called out again. He stopped, turned around, looked at me without response or recognition, and then went on his way, disappearing down a staircase.

The Sony said six twelve.

Then, suddenly, we were sitting beside the swimming pool at the Gregorys', Valerie, Aunt Margaret, Uncle Alfred, and myself. Alfred was pouring Bloody Marys from a pitcher. I could hear the low hum of conversation, point-less, indistinguishable. I glanced toward the pool. In the middle was Matthew Holbein, arms thrashing wildly about, calling "Dr. Pleier!"—or was it "Father"?—crying for me to save him. I tried to move but could not. Everyone else went on chatting indifferently as I watched in frozen horror.

Six thirty-eight on the Sony.

I awoke feeling drained. The wind was blowing in through the window, cooling the early morning air. Dimly, I could see dawn. It had been raining during the night, and leaves on the trees outside the bedroom window were still covered with droplets of water. Valerie lay in the bed next to me, sleeping. I reached over and touched her and felt reassured.

Downstairs in the kitchen, I fixed some instant coffee and put half-and-half in it. It was hard to shake off the confusion and disorientation of the dream. Thank God I didn't have many of them, I thought. How much better to jump out of bed in the morning after a dreamless night, refreshed, ready for anything, as I usually did. But I couldn't help running over the dream's details again as I sat there, wondering if I could find some meaning in them. They made no sense at all.

"Why are you up so early, darling?" Valerie stood in the doorway in her dressing gown, her eyes still half closed, but looking nonetheless appealing.

"Had a dream. Woke up. Just came down to have some coffee."

"Come back to bed."

"In a few minutes."

"Why not now?"

"I'm trying to sort some of it out."

She went to the refrigerator and poured herself a small glass of orange juice.

"Funny," I muttered. "Part of it took place at your Aunt Margaret's."

"Was I in it?"

"Yes."

"Did you love me?"

"In the dream?"

"Of course."

"Don't be silly."

"I'm not being silly. I just want to know whether, if you dreamed about me, you loved me. That's all."

"A dream is a dream is a dream."

"You're not answering my question."

"It's a silly question."

"I don't think it's silly at all." She had finished her juice and was washing the glass out in the sink. My coffee was half gone. "You're probably just miffed that Uncle Alfred didn't invite us to the country for the Labor Day weekend, that's all. And now it shows up in a dream." She grinned. "You psychiatrists are always looking for something deeper and missing the simplest explanations."

There was some truth in what Valerie was saying. I had gradually learned to compensate for the indoctrination I had received early on in my professional education— that one should always suspect that what the patient is saying is not really what he wants to say at all. It could be a one-way ticket to paranoia.

"Stop introspecting and come to bed."

"I'm not sleepy."

"That's not what I had in mind."

~6~

DAVE BRIXTON ASKED ME TO STOP BY HIS OFFICE THE NEXT morning. I did.

"No news about Matthew Holbein yet, I assume, or I would have heard about it," I said.

"Nothing."

There was a gentle knock at the door, and a young, blond woman of about twenty-eight, in a long white clinic coat, opened it and walked in.

Brixton stood up. "Fred, this is Dr. Lambert, one of our third-year residents. Dr. Lambert, Dr. Pleier."

"I've heard you lecture," she said. Her voice will make a lot of patients feel better in a hurry, I thought.

"I asked Dr. Lambert to take a special interest in the Holbein case. She has kept up contact with the family and has also maintained a pretty active involvement with the Missing Persons Bureau of the police."

"Nothing?" I asked, knowing the answer.

"Nothing about Matthew Holbein. But some interesting information has turned up. I sent some questions through on the library computer to the central data bank on the question of missing persons and escaped patients in particular. Do you want to see what I've come up with?"

She opened a manila folder and handed a long white-and-green printout sheet to Dave. He peered at it, obviously not knowing quite where to start reading, and said, "Why don't you just summarize it for us?"

"There are about twenty articles in the journals on the subject. Most of them are poorly done. But a couple"— she reached out and pointed to two places on the sheet— "Adams and Goldbaum and another by Smothin—are pretty good. They estimate that nearly five hundred thousand persons were reported missing in the United States each year during the last three years and that of these nearly a hundred thousand are never seen or heard from again. Even if half of these represent failure to report the person's return, that still leaves about fifty thousand people who never turn up. They also report that there are about three thousand hospital 'elopements' a year, during the last five years at any rate. About half the patients return to the hospital within two days, and another thirty-five percent simply go home."

"And the other fifteen percent?"

"Suicides account for only three percent. The police end up locating, directly or indirectly, about six percent. These are the ones who are found wandering around confused and those who find their way into some commune somewhere. The incidence of a true fugue state is almost infinitesimal—I think five cases reported in the five years of study."

A fugue state—forgetting who you are and taking on another identity—was something we learned about in medical school. I recalled being asked to define and discuss it on my specialty board examinations. But in twenty years of work I had never seen one, except on television.

Dr. Lambert went on. "That leaves about six percent unaccounted for."

"That sounds like a pretty big chance we may never find out what happened to Matthew." I felt a surge of hopelessness and puzzlement. "In this day and age of social security numbers and computers it's hard to see how such a large percentage could just vanish. It's one thing if you deliberately decided to move somewhere else and hide out, for some real reason, owing money, alimony, a crime of some kind, or maybe even just a thought-out change in life-style. But for such an identity change it seems to me you'd have to have your wits about you. To disappear in a state of marked disorganization and not show up again or be found seems extremely unlikely."

"Do either of these papers suggest an answer to the six percent who are never found?" Brixton asked.

"Only speculation," she replied.

"Do some of those who vanished, say, five years ago, show up later?" he asked.

"Of course," she said. "But then they're listed under the 'found' category. So the figure of six percent holds up across the board."

"What sort of speculations do the authors propose?" I asked, realizing the limited value of such suggestions in solving a particular disappearance.

"The usual. Concealed suicide, by swimming out to sea and drowning and the body not being found, for example. Or a sudden recovery from the acute psychotic episode, if that's what the patient had, and then a rational decision to depart for places unknown because family conditions are rotten."

"Six percent means about two hundred people a year. In five years, that's a thousand people!" Dave exclaimed.

"The police are unimpressed. They have even higher figures for total disappearances among people not identified as psychiatric patients."

"Still . . . it's an impressive number," Dave said.

"It's tough on the parents—the Holbeins, I mean." I thought of the fact that in the three months since Matthew's escape I'd talked with Frank only twice and with Cynthia not at all. They had persistently avoided me.

"I've spoken with them from time to time," Dr. Lambert said. "They are still quite upset."

"I don't blame them," said Dave. "It's like a son or husband missing in action, and you don't know whether they're alive or dead and the war ends and you still don't find out, even when the prisoner-of-war lists are finalized and a burial search is finished."

"You will keep on it?" I asked Dr. Lambert.

"Of course," she replied.

"Thank you, Dr. Lambert. That will be all," Dave said.

She turned to me. "It's been a pleasure to meet you, Dr. Pleier," she said.

The door closed after her, and Dave smiled. "I can see a lot of trouble with male patients and erotic transference in therapy with her."

I laughed automatically. His voice seemed far away. I couldn't stop thinking about the statistics. What the hell happens to all those people?

When I left Brixton's office, I headed for the taxi stand. I was supposed to meet Valerie for a quick lunch and a stop at Bloomingdale's to look at a pair of lamps we were thinking of buying for the living room. I walked past the taxis, around the south side of the clinic building, and along the narrow paved pathway that led to the pedestrian bridge spanning the highway and leading to the walk along the East River. It was a good day, I thought, for the several joggers who brushed past me—bright and crisp. The current flowed with October vigor. I stood there, staring at it, wondering, for no more than five or ten minutes that seemed like forever, what had really happened to Matthew. What had happened to all those people Dr. Lambert had been talking about?

"Your four-thirty appointment is canceled," Bernice said as I walked into my office after lunch. "Mrs. Warren. She'll be in next Thursday. One of her children has the flu."

I went into my office and sat down at the desk. Papers were strewn across it, but the appearance of disorderliness was deliberate rather than inadvertent. Total neatness, rather than making me feel more precise, seemed to give me a sense of trapped emptiness and sterility.

Shuffling through the folders and stacks of paper, I came across the Pleiert treatise. It had been sitting there ever since my return from Basel. Valerie had been fascinated by it but had asked me not to make too much of it. I wasn't likely to anyway. I was not well read in seventeenth-century European history, and so looking at the document and trying to imagine one Fridericus Pleiert as a student in Basel and a doctor in Worms in that period conjured up no images beyond the haunting portraits of Rembrandt and the familiar story of Martin Luther nailing his protests on the church door. (Or was that the sixteenth century?)

Nonetheless, I felt curious. I called Bernice on the intercom and asked her to step in.

"Bernice, I'd like you to hunt around and see if you can find someone who knows Latin, to translate this." I handed her the document. "You could call Columbia or maybe the Jesuits at Fordham. Tell whoever you find that we'll pay a reasonable fee and find out what you think it will cost."

Bernice was a gem. In her mid-fifties, she had never married and lived in Staten Island with her sister and the sister's family. She had begun working for me shortly before Caroline died. Later, I would joke with her about being my Jewish aunt, because she was always worrying about whether as a widower I was eating properly and getting enough sleep and seeing the right kind of women and suggesting activities to do with Lisa on weekends and in the summer. When I married Valerie, Bernice made it clear that she genuinely approved, though wistfully, knowing that the very fact of my good choice would mean I would have less need for her.

"And I'd like to write a letter to Worms."

"Worms?" She looked at me quizzically. "Is that a person or do you mean the city in Germany?"

"The city."

"I assume you have someone in particular in mind to address the letter to."

I thought a moment. I wasn't sure. "Address it to the Office of the Mayor. Hopefully, if there is a special record bureau or archives, they'll know what to do with it."

I dictated a brief letter, describing the document and requesting any information they might have about Fridericus. "And see if you can get me a map of Germany, Switzerland, and the Alsace."

"Where would I do that?"

"Brentano's. Doubleday's. One of those Michelin jobs that show everything in detail." Germany was a geographical blur for me. For curiosity's sake I wanted to see where Worms was. I hadn't been to Europe at all until the mid-sixties, after Caroline's death, and then I went to England and France and Spain, but not to Germany.

I wondered how far Worms was from Hechingen, or either of them from Basel. If there is a family connection, I thought, maybe some message was carried by the genes so that old Fridericus, failing to finish his work, communicated an anlage that was carried down, generation after generation, to reappear now, three hundred and fifty-odd years later, for some undefinable reason and because the circumstances were biologically appropriate.

Becoming a psychiatrist had been, for me, really quite coincidental. I had considered half a dozen careers besides medicine as an undergraduate, and my decision to specialize in psychiatry was made practically at the last minute after I had finished my medical internship at Bellevue. I stumbled into my interest in depression by accident. One of the first patients assigned to my care in the psychiatric pavilion happened to be suffering with a manic-depressive illness. I became fascinated with his treatment and gradually drawn into my own research studies. Maybe there was some genetic imprint matching up with seemingly random events to create a personal destiny—the sort of thing Carl Jung proposed in his theory of synchronicity.

"And Bernice. One more thing. Call the Public Library and get onto the genealogy people there. See if you can get a referral to someone who can do a family search in Germany. Oh, and find out, if you can, how much they think it might cost."

"What kind of afternoon did you have, darling?" Valerie called from the kitchen as I came in the front door.

"Routine," I answered. "And you?"

She literally danced into the hallway, gave me a big hug, and said, excitedly: "Wonderful. Full of solutions. After you left me at the store, they checked the warehouse—and the lamps we picked out will be here in ten days. Then, on my way home—you know, I got pretty well into my new story while you were away—I thought of a nice little piece of drama for a chapter ending, so I've wrapped it up, and after dinner, you can look at the first three chapters."

While she was talking she took me by the hand and led me into the kitchen. Jenny was lying on the floor, coloring, and stopped long enough to jump up and give me a hug.

"And another thing," Valerie said, "I've discovered you have a minor talent for prophecy."

"What does that mean?"

"Guess."

"I can't."

"Try."

"That stock we bought, what was it, Automatic Computer, has doubled."

"No, silly."

"Dorothy has decided to divorce Jack."

"Never. She likes to suffer too much."

"Hell, I don't know. What?"

"Aunt Margaret's invited us up for the weekend."

~7~

AS WE DROVE ALONG THE DRIVEWAY TO THE GREGORY HOUSE, I lost track of Valerie's voice for a moment. I was distracted by bits and pieces of my dream of several nights before. It was curiously reassuring when the final stretch of drive came into sight and, at the end of it, the white-clapboard house, looking exactly as it should. But the sight of the swimming pool covered with a tarpaulin sent a quick shudder through me—a fleeting memory of a boy calling my name. Margaret was waiting for us outside the doorway as we pulled up.

"Valerie. Frederic. I'm so glad you came early."

I had grown very fond of Aunt Margaret. After Valerie's parents had died, it was Margaret who had made a home for her. Now in her mid-seventies, she was as energetic as most women half her age and just as attractive, thanks to her restless, inquisitive mind combined with her natural grace. She had a rare warmth and generosity of heart.

I was fond of her husband, Alfred, too, but in quite a different way. Alfred was stiff, formal, aloof. Even though he meant well, smiling always seemed to require some effort for him, and when he spoke, it was briefly and to the point, still with a trace of his English accent, even though he had been in America since he was eight.

We lunched on the terrace.

"I hope you're not working too hard, Frederic," Margaret said.

"Work's my hobby, Margaret."

"I mean the kind of work you do. Being a psychiatrist. It must be a great strain at times."

"Fred's pretty careful," Valerie said. "He only spends a certain number of hours a week with patients."

"And I've quit just about every administrative or bureaucratic job I had. The patients are really much less of a strain than dealing with committees or trying to get programs through organizational roadblocks."

"I guess it's a matter of style. Alfred used to thrive on that."

Alfred forced a slight smile. In the late 1950s, before he became an undersecretary of state in the Eisenhower administration, he had sold his metallurgy plant for nearly eight million dollars. Some time later, although I was never exactly clear about his role, I knew that he had been a behind-the-scenes figure in the development of one of the major fast-food chains that had transformed the hamburger and french fries business. Now, at eighty-one, he divided his time between cataloging his rare book collection, attending directors' meetings of the various corporations in which he was involved, and just being with Margaret.

"Alfred's going to nap after lunch," said Margaret. "I've a few odds and ends to putter with. Why don't the two of you just relax? Cocktails at six, if that's all right.

I've invited some friends over for dinner. I think you'll find them interesting. Edward Markle and his wife, Charlotte. He's a film producer. Lives down the road. And Nancy Brighton. You remember her, Valerie. The decorator. Her husband died last year quite suddenly. Oh, and the Markles' house guest, who happens to be a psychiatrist too. You probably know him, Frederic. Adam Rheinhart?"

"Rheinhart," I said. "That's a coincidence. He spoke at the clinic just a few weeks ago." On the day Matthew disappeared, I remembered.

Nancy Brighton arrived first that evening. We were just about to take a second round of drinks when the Markles came in with Rheinhart.

"Frederic Pleier. Yes. Of course. We met a short while ago," Rheinhart said warmly.

The conversation moved quickly from topic to topic—some local zoning and environmental issues, politics, Nancy's decorating business—but returning most often to prices and the horrors of inflation. I was getting bored and decided to change the subject.

"Are you still lecturing here in the East?" I asked Rheinhart.

Ed spoke up quickly. "Adam's involved in some pretty interesting stuff."

"What is that?" Margaret asked. "Something new in psychiatry?"

Adam Rheinhart smiled. "Not exactly." He turned to me. "My lecture tour is over—I'll be off for California on Monday." Then he said to Margaret, "My subject is parapsychology. More specifically, reincarnation, in which I've become increasingly interested over the last ten years."

From the expression on his face, I could tell he knew that the first reaction would be an embarrassed silence, as if he had committed a social blunder.

Alfred, the ultimate in down-to-earth practicality, took longer than usual to produce one of his smiles. Valerie glanced at me. I knew she was thinking about the Basel document and was sending me a message that whatever I was about to hear should not be taken too seriously. She had no reason for concern.

"Do you really believe in reincarnation, Dr. Rheinhart?" Nancy Brighton asked.

"I don't believe in it, nor do I disbelieve," said Rheinhart clearly and slowly. "For a researcher, it's not a subject for faith. I try to approach it as dispassionately and scientifically as possible.

"Of course," he went on, "I know that using the word 'reincarnation' here in America produces skepticism, particularly among colleagues. I'm sure my academic position is still intact only because my fellow psychiatrists remember my more orthodox years and are simply amused by what they undoubtedly consider a middle-aged aberration."

I liked his being able to laugh at himself. "What exactly is your research approach?" I asked.

Rheinhart said, very precisely, "I am at present investigating certain aspects of hypnosis."

"Like Bridey Murphy—regressing people?" Valerie asked.

"Wait a minute!" Nancy broke in. "You're from California, right?" Rheinhart nodded. "And that's where they're doing that past-life therapy. A friend of mine was out there recently and was dying to try it, but she couldn't stay long enough. Do you . . . ?"

Rheinhart shook his head. "I've really had no first-hand contact with that kind of practice. But there are so many reports of people assuming other identities under the influence of hypnosis that have simply never been thoroughly or scientifically checked out—never could be. That doesn't mean they may not be valid, some of them, but even when the hypnosis is conducted under the most rigorous controls, the majority of the cases are hard to substantiate."

"There's some woman up in Oregon or Washington who hypnotizes people in groups," Alfred said, amusedly. "Read about it in one of the magazines at my barber's just last week."

Margaret, countering Alfred's muted sarcasm, said, "Wasn't that San Francisco, dear?" and turned to Adam with, "Is there any real evidence that people are reincarnated?"

"I think the work of Henry Henderson at Westport University in Connecticut affords, on the whole, the most impressive evidence so far." Rheinhart then described Henderson's research methods—systematically, patiently taking careful histories from young children who claimed to remember people and events from before they were born, and from places neither they nor their families had ever been, and then painstakingly checking the details and, in some cases, corroborating an incredibly high percentage of those details.

"Why such young children?" Valerie asked.

"They seem to be in closer touch with past lives than adults are," Rheinhart said. "Adults' minds, Henderson points out, become cluttered up with influences that may creep into supposed past-life personalities—one reason that he avoids hypnosis in favor of the spontaneous stories told by children." He went on to explain that a great deal of Henderson's work had been carried out in India, where, because of the traditional belief in reincarnation, parents would listen to their children's unusual stories and take them seriously.

"Can you imagine what would happen in the average American household," Rheinhart remarked in a lighter tone, "if Junior started babbling on about having once been an engineer on the Western Pacific Railroad when it was built across the prairies? Father would tell him he'd been watching too much television, and Mother would tell him to do his homework or go out and play."

I suddenly recalled Holbein's story of Matthew playing with his walled city.

"That's one thing that troubles me about reincarnation," Nancy was saying. "So many of the stories about it are reported in Eastern cultures. Isn't it possible that, precisely because they do believe in it, they make up stories to validate it?"

"I'm sure that often happens. But Henderson has several hundred cases of children in the United States as well, and the stories actually check out."

"Do they?" asked Alfred.

"I've gone over his materials myself," Rheinhart replied. "I've listened to his recordings. In my mind, there is little room to suspect the children have been prompted. They're quite spontaneous."

"What about your own work in hypnosis?" I asked. "You think more of that approach than Henderson does, apparently."

"Its potential is too great to turn our backs on, I feel. We are trying in our experiments to work out new and refined techniques. Which probably won't happen tomorrow. But there is a fascination . . . take a man who, when hypnotized, speaks in a language he cannot speak when conscious and who describes conditions of living two centuries ago in another country of which he is totally ignorant. This actually divides itself into two types of material—the foreign language, which excites us, and the purported names and other details that may be impossible to check out."

"And what is so exciting about the language?" Margaret asked.

"If it can really be established after exhaustive investigation that the person could not possibly have learned or been exposed to that language, it's some of the most impressive evidence for reincarnation that can be found. In parapsychology, the term for it is 'xenoglossy.' Such cases are very rare, alas, but the sort of thing that keeps us hoping."

I suggested the possibility of a genetic explanation.

"We haven't been able to establish one," Rheinhart replied. He smiled at me. "You're too much of a materialist, Frederic. Better take a look at what modern physics is saying about time and matter. They may be much more illusory than we have believed."

"I'll look into it," I said, smiling back. "How did you get interested in this type of work, Adam?"

"Accidentally, I suppose. Like yourself, Frederic, I was brought up traditionally in our field. About fifteen years ago I was called in as a consultant to evaluate a situation that apparently involved a poltergeist, and the idea of finding a rational explanation for such a phenomenon was a singular challenge."

"Poltergeist," muttered Alfred. "You mean things being thrown around and broken by some mysterious invisible force?"

"Precisely."

"Shades of demonology," said Alfred.

"Quite the contrary," said Rheinhart firmly. "The poltergeist is one phenomenon in which we have some important clues toward an explanation that can fit into a scientific framework."

Ed Markle spoke up. "That's how I met Adam. I was doing a story on the L.A. police who had called on Adam's group to look into a poltergeist attack. His group has an emergency team that rushes to the scene to see what can be done and carefully record the findings."

"We had an incident like that only last month, as a matter of fact," Adam went on. "The police called to tell us they had a poltergeist report from near Santa Monica. Dr. Carstairs, who works with us in this area, went to a house where an elderly woman and her fifteen-year-old grandson live together. When the police got there the place was a shambles. The kitchen had been literally destroyed by some force greater than a team of five men could muster. The sink was torn from the pipes. The refrigerator had been broken in half. It was incredible. The old lady and the boy were shivering with fear."

"And you suggest there's a scientific explanation for that?" I asked.

"We have a lead. Episodes such as this seem to occur in homes in which there is an emotionally disturbed adolescent. Not openly psychotic, you understand, but deeply troubled inside and concealing it. Our theory is that such intense psychological turmoil, which can neither be expressed nor resolved, somehow emerges as a violent physical disturbance, like the wreckage Carstairs saw and photographed in Santa Monica."

It occurred to me that Rheinhart was describing a dilemma at the core of psychosomatic medicine. While it was obvious that physical diseases, such as ulcers and high blood pressure, were linked to stressful life events, we still had no adequately substantiated modus operandi. Transduction. How could life problems register in the brain and then be converted into physical changes in the body?

Rheinhart was describing transduction on an even more complicated scale, since it involved the transformation of inner experience, intangible, into an energy force that could move mountains, or at least refrigerators.

"We may have a case of reincarnation right here in this room, Dr. Rheinhart," Alfred announced loudly. I was slightly annoyed. Valerie had obviously told Margaret about Fridericus.

Rheinhart said something like, "How interesting," but his expression revealed that he suspected he was being put on. However, politeness won out as he asked, "What do you mean?"

"You tell him, Fred," Alfred said.

I recounted the story of the document Heimwich had found in the Basel archives.

"The same name. The same subject matter," Rheinhart pondered aloud. "Curious, surely. A coincidence? Depending on where your forebears originated, perhaps."

"Pleier is not a common name, is it?" Ed Markle said. "I'd be pretty suspicious."

"Have you looked into the matter, Fred?" Rheinhart asked.

"Not really," I replied, still feeling uneasy that the subject of Heimwich's odd gift had been brought up in the context of our conversation. "Well, I did ask my secretary to see if she could get the treatise translated from the Latin."

"Maybe you are related through your family," Rheinhart said. "It wouldn't hurt to make a few inquiries." He thought a minute. "Have you tried to find a portrait?"

"A portrait?"

"Of old Pleiert. If he was the physician for the city of Worms in the seventeenth century, there just might be a portrait of him around."

For one instant, at the thought of standing in some old Gothic hall in a German town staring up at a painting of a figure garbed in black and seeing my own face looking sternly down at me, I went quite cold.

"It should be a lovely day tomorrow," Margaret said after the guests had left and we were getting ready to go upstairs to bed. "The two of you might want to play some tennis, and in the afternoon there's the horse show in Norwich. I hope you can stay over until Monday."

That night I had another nightmare, one that, when I awoke, I knew I would never want to tell to Valerie. I was lying on a bed, about to go to sleep, when my entire left side, from the top of my head to my toes, collapsed, flattened, and took on the texture of brown paper or canvas. My right side remained intact, and with great effort I could lift my right half from the mattress to sit up, pulling the left along. I awoke, frantic, in a half-upright position, and reached over to feel my left side to see if it was all right. It was.

Sitting quietly in the dark, I thought about the experience. Thank God it wasn't a stroke. The right side of the brain governs the left side of the body and the left side of the brain governs the right. The left brain is the site of logic and intellect. The right brain is the seat of imagination, intuition, visual imagery. Could it mean that my more logical self was dying and my more imaginative self was assuming command? Transduction. We had talked about that. How do the mind and body connect? Descartes had split them, and few people believed in the idea of an immaterial soul anymore.

My mind suddenly jumped to Rheinhart's question about a portrait of "old Pleiert," and my reasoning stopped abruptly. Fear overwhelmed me as I realized that in the dream my left side had not only had the texture of canvas. It had been, in fact, an oil painting of myself, and for one instant I felt possessed by a spirit that was truly not my own.

~8~

SEX HAD PLAYED A BIG PART IN DRAWING VALERIE AND ME to each other. We had met by chance at a ski club that a good friend of mine belonged to. I was an amateur skier myself, restricting my adventures to the junior and intermediate slopes and usually quitting early in the afternoon, before it became too cold and any ice could form. On that particular afternoon the club's coffee shop was nearly empty. Everyone was on the slopes. As I sat there, sipping hot chocolate and reading a World War II spy story—I can't recall the name—I looked up and spotted Valerie sitting near a window watching the thin line of skiers, dots in the distance, moving down the white hillside. Even though she was bundled up in a thick yellow jacket and black ski pants and boots, I could see that she was indeed a beautiful woman—brown-haired, fair-skinned, and with features that would make most models envious. And yet she looked alert and warm and very real.

I had never been the type to walk over to a stranger and just introduce myself there and then. But I was so struck by Valerie that I was determined to find a way to meet her. As luck would have it, my friend knew her casually, so when he stomped into the shop, ordered coffee, and sat down with me, I told him what was on my mind, and he promptly took me over to say hello. He had tried to take her out a few times himself, he warned me, but had gotten nowhere.

Sexual attraction is a complicated business. There are few objective standards, and those are highly cultural and very susceptible to changing times. It's the individual preferences that are mysterious and that begin so early in life. I recall that in my adolescence, in daydreams and in films, a certain type of woman appealed to me more than any other. I don't know where the image came from. It obviously was sexual, but much more was involved; it was an image of someone to play hero to, but someone to share with as well; someone to sit with by a warm fire on a cold December day and hold hands with and talk to and listen to. Someone to make love with, intensely, sensually, and in the end become one with, lovingly.

Valerie was really the first woman I had ever met who corresponded to that daydream. And as we came to know each other in every way, over the year following that chance encounter, the similarity between my image and the reality revealed by our growing closeness became indistinguishable. It was about then that my recurrent dream of searching for a particular room in a particular house disappeared. For Valerie as well, I must have represented something buried deeply within her, judging by the way her attraction to me and love for me seemed to parallel mine for her, but what it was I never knew. It was something she simply never talked about.

Not that we never disagreed. Once in a while an argument might arise suddenly, seemingly over nothing at all, and assume a theatrical quality. But this didn't happen often and seldom lasted very long, and we were both resolute in our purpose of never saying good night on an unpleasant note.

But sex and openness had become so much a part of our day-to-day life that any shift in this balance would be rather quickly noticed. So it was small wonder that one night about two weeks after our return from the Gregorys', during which we had not made love once, Valerie, lying in bed in the darkness, asked me whether something was wrong.

"What do you mean?"

"We haven't made love in over two weeks. And the few times I indicated some interest, you've ignored me." There was no tone of accusation in her voice, only gentle concern.

"I'm sorry. I hadn't noticed."

"Have I done something?"

"Of course not." I reached out and took her hand. "It's not you," I said. "It's me. And it's not sex. It seems to be everything. A kind of malaise. But I'm pulling out of it."

Valerie turned on the bedside lamp. I sat up. She got out of bed, walked across the room, took a cigarette from her dresser, and lit it as she sat down on the large chair, where she could face me.

"I'm really getting worried, Fred. You haven't been yourself since the summer . . . not since that Holbein case."

"I went to see Mort Stein," I replied defensively, "just as I promised. He didn't seem to think there was anything seriously the matter."

"Well, you still seem different. Margaret noticed

it too. That's why she told you she hoped you weren't working too hard."

"You're assuming that!"

"No. We've talked about it."

"I don't like the idea of your talking with Margaret or anyone about me that way," I said angrily.

"Fred, please. You know better than that. You know I love you and Margaret loves you. I wouldn't discuss it with anyone else."

"You make it sound as if I'm really losing my grip."

"Of course not. It's just that you've been terribly preoccupied. Last night, at dinner, I don't think you said more than three sentences."

"I was listening to you."

"That's not the point. If you are under some kind of strain, please, darling, share it with me."

"There's nothing you're not already aware of."

"All right, then. Maybe it's something you don't recognize. Maybe you should go back to Stein and talk it out some more. That's what you're always recommending to everyone else."

"You're not suggesting I go back into analysis, I hope!"

"You could see him a few times."

"I told you, he said everything was fine," I replied. In fact, thinking back, I couldn't recall that Mort had made any comment on how he thought things were going, one way or the other.

"It's just that I love you so much and I need you so much, I can't bear the thought of anything happening to you or to us."

Valerie stood up, walked over to the bed, and lay

down next to me, pressing her body against mine. "I want you now," she whispered.

"Me too."

The next morning at breakfast, I was unusually cheerful.

"I'm really sorry about the last few weeks. Val. I'll work on it."

She poured a second cup of coffee for each of us.

"There is something I didn't mention last night, Fred. But I have to get to it. It's this Fridericus business. I hope you're not beginning to take it seriously. Finding that document and running into Rheinhart at Margaret's, they were curious coincidences. But that's all. I hope that is not what is eating at you."

"Don't be ridiculous. You know me better than that."

"Do I?"

"Of course you do. And even if there were something to it, what difference would it make anyway? I certainly don't remember any previous life. This is the only life anyone knows, and it's difficult enough as it is. Who would want to come back? Except to be with you, naturally."

She grinned but refused to be sidetracked. "Still, it's just the kind of thing that could get out of hand if you let it. I know you well enough to know that if your curiosity gets aroused or if you get interested in something, you can pursue it with a passion until it's settled."

"Well, I haven't gone over the edge yet. Besides, if I do, they have all kinds of miracle drugs nowadays to pull me out of it." I was trying to be amusing, but Valerie wasn't buying it.

80

"Sometimes I wish you were in a field that didn't involve delving into people's minds—and your own."

"Like Alfred and his hamburger stands?"

"There's something to be said for counting the number of burgers you sell each month instead of living in a sea of intangibles. Please don't misunderstand—I know how much your work means to you. I know how much good you do. It's just that I can see how it all could get to someone as perceptive and sensitive as you are."

"I'll watch out. Don't be concerned."

"More coffee?"

"No, thanks."

"Have you looked into this Fridericus business any further?" She asked the question casually, not even looking at me.

"No," I answered with equal casualness.

I lied, something I had never done with Valerie before. Not only had I written to Worms and set in motion a preliminary investigation into my own family origins; I had already received some answers and had begun to do some reading on seventeenth-century Europe.

The letter from Worms had been brief and to the point:

Herr Professor Pleier:
    We regret that we are limited with regard to the information that we can supply you about Fridericus Pleiert, since the City of Worms was destroyed many times since his time and many of our records are gone, particularly during the fire of 1689. [I subsequently learned that the fire to which they referred was, in fact, the doing of the Sun King, Louis XIV, when he chose to

destroy all the cities in the Rhine Palatinate.]
Nonetheless, we are able to give you the
following. Pleiert is mentioned as godfather in
archive records: 15 Mar. 1628, 17 May 1640,
23 Aug. 1640 and 1 Mar. 1641. Dr. Pleiert's wife
Anna Katherine is mentioned as godmother 14
Mar. 1626 and 30 July 1630. Also mentioned
is a Christina as Dr. Pleiert's wife, 6 Aug. 1633.
[So, Pleiert was married twice, the second time
somewhere between 1630 and 1633.]
Marriage records in Worms begin only in
1657, and death records since 1682. Birth
records have existed since 1604, but have a gap
from 1642 to 1672.
Prior to his arrival in Worms, in 1623, Pleiert
had been Physician to the City of Mulhouse. We
suggest you inquire there. As to any portrait [I
had sent a telex about this after Adam
Rheinhart's suggestion] we have no record
whatsoever.

Hans Kohler
Archivist

I had also taken a few minutes one afternoon to
peruse a road map of Germany in an old guidebook and
was startled to discover the small distances that separated
Worms, Mulhouse, Basel, Strasbourg, and Hechingen,
places where old Fridericus had presumably studied or
worked. And Hechingen, my grandfather had told me, was
the town where my family had originated. The entire area
could not be much larger than the state of New Jersey.
The Rhine flowed past Worms, and you could trace it down
(against its flow, of course) past Strasbourg on the French
side to Basel, with Mulhouse a few miles northeast. Hechingen was on the other side of the river, east of Strasbourg
and between the Black Forest and the Swabian Jura.
When I arrived at the office about nine thirty, Bern-

ice was already there, and after we had taken care of some business correspondence, she handed me a large envelope which had arrived by special delivery. It was postmarked France. Inside was a gray-covered journal, entitled *Bulletin du Musée Historique de Mulhouse,* Tome LXI—Année 1953. The table of contents was printed right on the cover. A red mark had been placed next to an article on page 65 titled, "Les médecins et chirurgiens de Vieux-Mulhouse." Next to the mark was the number 104.

I turned to page 104.

> Friedrich Pleiert, né à Worms vers 1595, mort à Worms après 1639. Imm. Strasbourg 1616; Heidelberg 1617; Bâle 1619. Thèse 1619: "De chlorosi seu morbo virgeneo." Thèse 1620: "De melancholia et idiopathica et sympathica." Dr. med. Bâle 8.6.1620. Médecin de la ville de Mulhouse 1620–1623. Prend son congé le 27.8.1623. Premier médecin de la ville de Worms en 1639. Marié le 4.6.1621 à Anna Katherine Wurstisen, de Bâle.

Bernice had translated the German communication from Worms for me before letting me struggle with it. But she knew no more French than I did. Nonetheless, the brief passage was not too difficult to figure out in general. Fridericus had been a student in Strasbourg, Heidelberg, and Basel. He'd been born in Worms around 1595 and died there after 1639. For three years he had been the physician for the city of Mulhouse and thereafter of Worms. On June 4, 1621, he married a woman from Basel named Anna Katherine Wurstisen.

It was very little, of course, but as I read it, for the first time I began to sense the reality of Fridericus. He was someone who had, in fact, lived and worked and married and died.

I had also begun to learn something of the world

in which he had lived, and it was not a very pretty place. When I had first learned of his existence, I pictured the man walking through the old streets of Basel, wearing a long robe, perhaps with a gold medallion around his neck, living in one of the small houses near the Petersgasse, with the colorful decorations painted above the doors, sitting with his colleagues arguing about the teachings of Galen and the controversies surrounding Paracelsus, who had preceded him by less than a century.

But as I read a historian's description of that time in history, I was appalled. From 1618, when Fridericus was in Heidelberg, until 1648, several years after his reported death, the Thirty Years War had raged throughout Germany, and the population of the Rhineland had been literally devastated by war, siege, slaughter, starvation, and recurrences of plague. Oddly enough, it was the dramatic and awful nature of the history of that period that stimulated my curiosity more intensely than the coincidence that someone with a name and interest similar to my own had lived at that time. Until this point, the Thirty Years War and the Hundred Years War and the War of the Roses and all the other wars that recurred throughout European history had been nothing but ill-defined phrases, indistinguishable from one another, in my mind. I could feel myself becoming fascinated with the chain of events, which gave me new insight into contemporary shifts of power and politics and increasingly convinced me of what historians already knew, that man's worst enemy seemed to be man.

I had a ten-thirty appointment with Janet Chambers. Janet was a tall, somewhat stocky woman in her late thirties who had first consulted me a year earlier because of tension headaches. She had just finished telling me about an incident in which she had successfully confronted her boss with her own need for more independence of action at work when she paused, loked at me quite earnestly, and said, "You're not listening."

"Of course I am."

"No, you're not. I don't like to criticize you and this isn't criticism. You know me well enough to know that. But you are somewhere else."

"What makes you think that?" It was an instinctive reaction. I found myself slightly annoyed at using the proverbial psychiatrist's maneuver of turning a conversation around with a question. But I also found myself quite sincerely wanting to know the answer. It seemed an echo of Valerie's concern.

"What was I just talking about?"

"Work."

"What about it?"

"You were going into some of the details of the kinds of responsibility you've been taking on. Like trying to reorganize that scholarship funding program."

"Frederic Pleier. That was ten minutes ago. I've been talking about how the woman I work under has a great need to control everything and how I tried to talk with her about it and get her to let me take on more by myself."

It sounded vaguely familiar.

"You've been staring out that window, and when you do look at me, it's as if you are looking right past me."

"I'm sorry. I must have been distracted."

"I hope there's nothing wrong," she said, genuinely concerned. There isn't really too much truth to the old adage that psychiatric patients end up either in love with or hating their doctors or a combination of both called

85

ambivalence, at least unless both the patient and therapist expect and encourage it. More often, as the patient becomes less self-centered because things are going better, he or she and the doctor will find themselves in a very real situation of friendship. And Janet Chambers's remarks were precisely that, the concern of a friend.

"Nothing at all, Janet, I assure you."

After she had gone, however, I continued to be somewhat distressed by her observation. To be sure, one's attention flags from time to time; nothing special about that. But Janet was too shrewd to react to a slight lapse in concentration. The chances were that she had noted something else, but either did not wish to say what or could not define it well enough to put it into words.

Charlie Clark, whom I had known on and off for a number of years and who had stopped by for an appointment that evening at five thirty for the first time in six months, had no trouble putting it into words.

"You look awful, Fred. Your eyes look exhausted. And I've never seen you so restless. What the hell is going on?"

"Nothing."

"Don't give me that crap. You look the way I did before I landed up in the hospital twenty years ago. For Christ's sake, you'd better do something about yourself. We need you."

Walking home that evening, I began to become really concerned. Three people in a row in one day telling me I looked badly. But I really didn't feel that badly. I suddenly remembered the psychiatrist in Noel Coward's *The Astonished Heart*, denying to everyone that anything was wrong with him and jumping out a window in the final scene. But then, he'd been having a hopeless love affair.

Maybe it's something physical, I thought. I'll call George McLaughlin and have him check me out. Next week. I have been feeling a little tired lately. He can check my blood pressure and heart and go over me thoroughly. But from the moment I thought of George, I could feel my resolve dwindling. Doctors are just like everyone else; we hate to go to other doctors lest they find something wrong with us we hadn't suspected.

~ 9 ~

I DID CALL GEORGE MCLAUGHLIN THE NEXT DAY AND WENT to see him that afternoon. He found everything very much in order.

"You're in pretty good shape, Fred. You probably could use a little more exercise. Weight good. Pressure good. When you have a chance, you might let me arrange for you to have a stress cardiogram, but your EKG looks fine. I won't have the blood tests back for a few days, but they're not likely to show much. Your only complaint is tiredness?"

"Some. But not enough to explain why Valerie and a few others have been telling me I don't look as well as you say I am. I have been having some trouble sleeping, getting to sleep, waking up a couple of times during the night, but that's all."

George looked up from the notes he was making and reached for a prescription blank. "Must be stress. Why not take some Dalmane for a few nights? Help you sleep."

"I'm not crazy about sleeping pills."

"Just take it for a week or so. Let me be the doctor. And try to get more physical activity."

I left George's office greatly relieved. He was a good doctor, and if he had found nothing physically wrong, it was unlikely that anyone else could either. But now that I had begun to plan to check things out and get back in shape, I decided to go all the way. I stopped at a phone booth on the corner of Madison and Seventy-second Street, dropped in a dime, and dialed Morton Stein. I knew the number by heart. The phone rang a half-dozen times, and I was about to hang up and try again when his answering service came on.

"Dr. Stein's office—one moment, please . . ." A click and then silence. I hated that. It was typical of every answering service I'd known, including my own. The bored voice returned. "Can I help you?" Dr. Stein, she thought, might be busy with a patient. But then again he might be out of town. Or maybe he's retired and you don't know it, I thought. I felt like saying that I had collapsed in the middle of Madison Avenue and had crawled to the phone and needed help right away, anything to jolt her out of her professional indifference. Instead, I left my name and number and the time when I could be reached.

Mort called an hour later and agreed to see me at seven that evening. I phoned Valerie to tell her I'd be late for dinner and why. She sounded relieved.

"Well," said Mort, "I didn't expect to see you again so soon."

"I didn't expect to be here."

We took our usual places. I told him that Valerie and a few others had suggested I wasn't looking well.

"You look all right to me," he said.

"I did have a good night's sleep last night."

"Have you been having trouble sleeping?"

"Some. Nothing dramatic."

"Well, how about you? Do you think you aren't in good shape?"

"I don't really know what to say. I do feel a bit out of sorts at times. Irritable. And maybe you could say that I have been slightly preoccupied, less sharp than usual."

"Preoccupied with what?"

"Nothing. Really. Everything seems to be okay now."

"Any more dreams?"

I knew he'd ask that. I told him about the nightmare in which half of me flattened into a painting. "That's the last one. I don't dream much. You know that. But this time I didn't even have one last night to get ready to see you. Maybe that's because I didn't decide to come until this morning."

"Sex?"

"Valerie did complain—complain's not a fair word—say that we hadn't been close that way for a couple of weeks."

"That's the second time you've quoted others to tell me what's going on. Was Valerie right?"

"Apparently."

"Then why not say so yourself?"

I felt as if he were being a bit picky. "I guess you could say my libido was less than usual."

"How have your spirits been?"

"All right. I get down sometimes, but it doesn't last long. Doesn't everyone?"

"Fred Pleier. You sound like someone who's never been to a psychiatrist before and is only here because someone told you to come and has to deny any sign of distress to prove to me that you are not troubled."

He looked concerned. We sat there silently for a minute that seemed to stretch on interminably. Suddenly I felt like crying. I didn't. But Mort spotted the change in my expression.

"You're really afraid, aren't you, Fred?" We were both thinking the same thing. "You're afraid you might go into a depression again."

A return of the kind of depression that had swept in on me after Caroline's and my father's deaths was something to fear: moments of pure panic, calling Mort two or three times a week for reassurance even though I was seeing him practically every other day; waking up at four in the morning feeling utterly hopeless; lying in bed at times, fighting a crazy urge to rush over to the window and leap out onto the sidewalk ten stories below; waiting, waiting, waiting for the antidepressant to take hold.

The whole experience had lasted only a month in its intense form, but that month had seemed like an eternity. Afterward, I felt like a patient recovering from severe pneumonia, making a great effort to be with people and pick up the pieces of my work, falling asleep uncontrollably over dinner in friends' homes. And I ached with loneliness.

"Certainly I'm afraid. Wouldn't you be?"

"But there's nothing going on in your life now that could trigger such a reaction." It was more a question than a statement.

"Nothing. You know things are going well. We discussed that just a short while ago."

The trouble with being both psychiatrist and patient is that you can spot the therapist's strategies as quickly as he devises them. Mort was now about to take a reassuring tack.

"You know as well as I that anyone who has been through a serious and painful depression will be afraid of going through the hurting again. And that even a period of slight stress, if it causes some tension or discouragement or frustration, will almost automatically stir up that fear."

"True." And even though I knew what he was doing, attempting to dispel my underlying fear, it was working. I could feel some lifting in my spirit.

"Of course, you're the one who advocates episodes of depression from time to time throughout life as a springboard for further growth."

"Sure. But not to be sought out. And not to be experienced in the absence of traumatic events." He was trying to provoke me to get to the root of the current problem.

He lit a cigarette, stood up, walked to the window, then turned around and looked at me earnestly. "Well, could it be biological?"

"What do you mean?"

"That's your field more than mine. Hormones. Minerals and the like. But I was wondering whether you think you might be mildly cyclothymic, with a recurrence of depressive symptoms without any outside stimulus. A sort of biological clock mechanism."

Mort Stein was committed to psychotherapy, but he was equally committed to staying up to date in his field. His question was sincere. So was his reference to my expertise. And his intent was obvious, to dig out any and all concerns that I might have about myself which, whether relevant or not, would subliminally make any state of tension I might be experiencing that much worse.

"I will be forty-five next April."

"Really getting on," he said, smiling. Mort was seventy-one.

I thought for a moment. "I'm not really so much depressed as afraid. Even afraid may be too strong a term. But I don't know of what."

"Why don't you go on and tell me whatever occurs to you?" said Mort, setting the stage for clarification.

"I have noticed one pattern that puzzles me," I said, after a few minutes.

"What's that?"

"The tension I feel, and the sleeplessness. Even the couple of nightmares I've had always seem to crop up when I've taken some steps to look into this seventeenth-century business."

"Old Fridericus?"

"Yes. It didn't occur to me as a pattern until this afternoon, when I knew I'd be seeing you. I'm still not sure."

"What has developed since you were here last?"

I told Mort about encountering Adam Rheinhart at the Gregorys' and about the information I had received from Worms and Mulhouse.

"Not much to go on, really," he said. "Don't you agree?"

"Not much at all." Suddenly I had a thought, flashing into my mind, irrelevant, insane, absurd.

Mort noticed the look of puzzlement on my face. "What is it?"

"A foolish connection."

"No connection is foolish. It may not be valid but it's not foolish. What is it?"

"Fridericus died at forty-four or forty-five. I'm that old now." I was embarrassed. "Dumb. Right?"

"What it tells us is that this thing is having more of an influence on you than you care to admit."

"I'm always willing to find out."

"That's easy enough to say. But it sounds to me as though this series of coincidences is starting to create a phobic and obsessive kind of trend, an urge to pursue it and at the same time a good deal of anxiety when you do. That could account for your periodic insomnia and for your preoccupation."

"Maybe. I didn't think I was taking it that seriously."

"Apparently, at some level, you are." Mort looked at his clock, perched on the bookcase where ordinarily his patients could not see it. It was seven thirty.

"Time up?" I asked.

"Not yet. It's worth a few more minutes. Tell me, have you made any other investigation into it?"

I couldn't be sure why I hesitated, but I did hesitate. Then I said, "I had his thesis on depression translated."

"Was it revealing?" Mort asked.

"Not really. Well . . . it's hard to say. It was remarkable how much he, and I suppose others, knew about depression in those days. Of course, they used the term to describe a multitude of mental ills. There are some bizarre descriptions of delusions, a patient who thought his buttocks were made out of crystal and was afraid to sit down and another who thought his nose was the size of an elephant's trunk and would never approach anyone else closer than five or six feet lest he injure him."

"Freud would have had a field day with those." Mort smiled.

"On the whole, his criteria for depression were pretty much the same as ours. Fear. Sadness. Trouble sleeping. Appetite loss. Weight loss. Loss of sexual interest. He could have written the list of indications for any antidepressant medication today. Even his analysis of causes is contemporary. Stress. He doesn't call it that, but

94

he lists the importance of grief and personal changes and jealousy and other feelings in his discussion of etiology. He even talks about pollution in the atmosphere and bad dietary habits."

"Very contemporary indeed. How much do you know of medical history, Fred?"

"A bit. I've read Zilboorg and a few articles. But I never took it on as a specialized area of interest."

"I do read medical history extensively . . . and if you had, you'd realize that some of his thinking as you describe it is remarkably advanced for the period in which he wrote. The humoral theory was still dominant even then."

"He did elaborate on vapors and humors—quite a bit, as a matter of fact."

"But what you're telling me suggests he saw beyond that. Was there anything else in the document? Anything that disturbed you?"

"Not really. Nothing that would ordinarily have bothered me. But . . . under the circumstances . . . he did go into some detail about the possible meaning of dreams, even of the rantings and ravings of patients. Suggested that they might . . . sometimes . . . have insights into a timeless stream of knowledge."

"Any references to himself?"

"Only one. Plenty of accolades to his teachers and others whose works seem to have influenced his thinking. But only one reference to himself." I could feel myself growing tense.

"What was that?"

"In the case of a patient who was convinced he was a Roman emperor, Pleiert asked whether, indeed, the delusion might have been rooted in a fragile sense of some other existence. Then he has a sentence in which he wonders if all of us, including himself, might not have had some prior life. He seemed convinced that the human spirit was eternal."

Mort was silent for a moment. Then he asked whether I had done anything to track down my own family background.

I had, of course. "Arranged for a genealogical group to look into it."

"And did you find anything out?"

"They were able to trace the Pleiers back to the 1780s, in Hechingen, to a Dominicus Pleier. But they haven't been able to find his birth record in the church there, so he may have emigrated from somewhere else. Most of the Pleiers were masons, and from what I've read, masons traveled quite a bit through that part of Europe, depending on what kind of building may have been going on. The Hohenzollern Castle, belonging to the family later giving rise to Frederick the Great and the kings of Prussia, originated there. It's in a mountainous area called the Swabian Jura. They did a lot of rebuilding of the original castle in the eighteenth and nineteenth centuries."

"That leaves a gap of nearly a hundred and fifty years between the time this Fridericus died and the earliest record of your own family. It is intriguing."

I could feel myself beginning to tremble inside. A wave of ill-defined anguish swept up through my body. I told Mort.

"What do you think triggered it?" he asked.

"Your reaction. When you said 'intriguing.' As if you were starting to take it seriously."

"Well, it is intriguing. But don't get the idea that I'm taking it seriously except as it affects you. Genealogical studies are one thing. But the occult . . ."

His word startled me.

"The occult, reincarnation, spirits, whatever you want to imply, there isn't a shred of firm evidence of anything like that in scientific literature. And you know that."

"And Rheinhart's work?"

"The application of experimental methodology to an overworked imagination. I knew him quite well, you know, or maybe you didn't. I was a service chief at Hopkins when he did his residency there. Bright young man. Great promise. A fine psychiatrist. But always given to outlandish ideas. I recall he once did a review paper on Carl Jung's explorations into astrology—during his residency years— and read it at a staff conference. I never could figure out how such a sound mind could be drawn into such baseless speculation."

Mort Stein's direct attack on Rheinhart instantly made me feel sure of myself again.

"You weren't beginning to give him any credence, were you, Fred?"

"Not at all. Not consciously, at any rate. No, not at any level."

It was a quarter to eight.

"I'll tell you what I think. What you have uncovered so far is really quite interesting, historically speaking. And I'm a big enough believer in looking into such curiosities that ordinarily I would say, fine, go ahead. But obviously this business is getting to you in some way. Like a fear of flying or closed spaces. As long as the phobic person avoids the object of his fear, he's fine. If he forces himself to take airplanes or subways, he will get anxious. I suppose if we wanted to be perfectionistic about it we'd get you back in serious analysis for a while and try to figure out the source of your anxiety and resolve it. And if you were a professional historian or serious student of parapsychology"—he smiled—"which you are not, we might have to do that or get some of that new behavioral conditioning therapy to help you overcome your fears."

He stopped for a moment and looked toward the window. Even though it was dark outside, we could both see the first sprinkle of snow starting to fall.

"Maybe we'll have a white Thanksgiving," he said. Then he continued. "A traveling salesman with a fear of trains and planes can't function. Neither can a coal miner with a fear of being trapped in small spaces. But there are millions of people with phobias that do not affect their life-style one bit. They can just avoid whatever it is that is stirring them up. And that's what I think you should do. Drop it. You've gotten enough out of your search. Put your papers in a back file and chalk it up to a brief encounter with the seventeenth century."

"Drop it?"

"Just that. Let it go."

The idea of giving up annoyed me, just on principle. I didn't like the thought of quitting any project or effort just because it stirred up some tension. It seemed like refusing to play a game of tennis because you lost more often than you won. I told Mort how I felt.

"This isn't a tennis game," he said, sternly. "Do you want to go back into analysis or run the risk of getting really upset again?" he added.

"Obviously not."

"You want my advice and I'm giving it to you. Drop it."

~ 10 ~

I TOOK THE DALMANE FOR A FEW NIGHTS, AS GEORGE McLaughlin had suggested, and I decided to take Mort Stein's advice as well. Bernice filed whatever information we had gathered thus far in one of the long rows of gray file cabinets that lined her office, under P for Pleiert. Janet Chambers noted, a couple of weeks later, that I was looking much fitter. I made some comment about sleeping better and she said that that was great and that we could now get on with the business of helping her cope.

Margaret and Alfred joined us for Thanksgiving dinner. The snow hadn't lasted, but it was a bright, crisp day with a chill in the air and a hint of winter in the sky.

Time is a funny thing. As a child the distance between starting school and Thanksgiving seems incredibly great and between Thanksgiving and Christmas almost interminable. But as you grow older, especially after forty, the months race by, seasons blurring into one another. There is never enough time for whatever it is you want to do, and every time you turn around it's Christmas again or summer or your birthday, or someone's graduation when it seems he or she had just started at that school.

Perhaps it's a question of familiarity. The suspense is removed. The distances are no more or less, nor is the time required to transit them. But subjectively, within the mind, everything becomes compacted, shortened, crowded together.

I had occasionally wondered, in the course of my work with patients and my research in depression, what is real time? For the person caught in the grip of hopelessness, slowed down by a mood of futility, withdrawing from contact with the outer world, time passes with singular, painful neverness. It will never be tomorrow. By contrast, for one in good spirits, stimulated, excited, moving, the day is over before it seems to have begun. Is the real time the steady clicking of a quartz watch, second by second? Or is the real time a perceptual experience, dependent largely on conscious and unconscious happenings within the individual?

This was the eighth Christmas Valerie and I had spent together married. On Christmas Eve, we took Lisa and a sleepy Jennifer to a special midnight service at Holy Trinity Church, where a good friend of mine was the minister. We had a large tree crowned with a silver angel, and on Christmas morning we came downstairs to open the presents, first those from friends, then those from family, and finally from each other. At nearly the last minute I had found a lovely bracelet of semiprecious stones and matching earrings for Valerie. She gave me a tape recorder and two airline tickets to Quebec for the New Year's holiday.

A week later, as the bells in the churches announced the beginning of the New Year, Valerie and I stood on the terrace of the Château Frontenac, looking out over the frozen St. Lawrence glistening in the moonlight. Behind us, through the large windows, we could see the grand ballroom and the couples dancing to the Lester Lanin sound, stopping long enough to blow horns and whirl noisemakers around and around as a cloud of multicolored balloons floated gently down from the ceiling.

"Happy New Year, darling," Valerie shouted, hugging me, then letting go and standing away while holding my hands in hers. "You give me so much joy," she said softly.

"Life would have no meaning for me without you, Val."

"I wish we could take moments like this and hold on to them forever, like a photograph that we could take out of an album, and relive them whenever we wanted," she said.

I took her in my arms and kissed her.

Three months later, by sheer accident I discovered that Valerie had planned a surprise party for my birthday. Margaret had called the office, perhaps in a moment of mild mental lapse, and left a message with Bernice to the effect that she and Alfred could not get there until eight. Bernice unsuspectingly told me. Putting this fact together with Valerie's insistence that I be home promptly at seven thirty, no earlier and no later, gave the secret away.

It was a quarter to five. I had just finished with a patient and was going over a few notes when Bernice knocked and walked over to my desk.

"A messenger just brought this down," she said. "It was addressed to you at the hospital and Dr. Brixton must have thought it was important enough to send on right away."

She handed me a white envelope, postmarked Basel.

The return address was that of Professor Heimwich. Our visit together the previous September seemed ages ago. No doubt he was sending me some follow-up information regarding our conference.

"Just one minute, Bernice. Let me see if this needs an answer."

His letter did cover some of the later reactions of various participants at the meeting we had had. It ended with cordial regards and a P.S. "I thought you might be interested in seeing what has turned up on F. Pleiert," he wrote in his own handwriting.

There was a sheet of Xeroxed paper accompanying his letter. At the top was a list of medical students matriculated at the University of Basel in 1619. Below that was a list of the various theses that each of the students had prepared and a brief biographical note on each student.

I handed the letter and enclosure to Bernice.

"File them," I said, firmly. But just as she was about to leave the room, I called her back.

"Wait a minute—just leave them here. I'll take a quick look before I go home or in the morning, and you can file them tomorrow."

I put them in my pile of things to be taken care of and readied myself for my five o'clock appointment. At seven, as I was about to turn off the lights to leave, my eye was caught by Heimwich's envelope on my desk. For an instant I could hear Morton Stein's voice saying, "Drop it," but I could feel the curiosity welling up in me like the urge for a cigarette that a smoker who is trying to stop must feel again and again during the first days of abstinence.

I glanced down the list of students. There was Pleiert. The biographical note that followed his name afforded me no new information. I felt relieved.

But then my eye caught a handwritten note at the bottom of the page: "We have discovered that Fridericus Pleiert had three children: Matthius, b. 25 Dec. 1622; Maria, b. 8 Nov. 1626; Katherine, b. 16 Jan. 1633. Prof. Heimwich."

As I read the names I felt my somewhat remote interest give way to a sickening sense of dread. I dropped the paper to the floor, reached down and groped to pick it up again, and reread it.

A son named Matthius, born on December 25, 1622, Christmas. The same first name as Matthew Holbein and the identical birthday.

What the hell was going on? Could this be some kind of joke that Brixton had cooked up with Heimwich's complicity? Not likely. Old Heimwich would never cooperate with a practical joke. Maybe the handwritten postscript wasn't Heimwich's at all, but Brixton's. He had opened the envelope at the hospital, scribbled the note at the end of Heimwich's enclosure, and then forwarded the doctored material to my office. I reached for the phone. No answer at Brixton's office. I called his home.

"What the hell do you think you're doing?" I asked, clutching the receiver tightly in my hand.

"What are you so upset about, Fred?"

"You know what I'm talking about. That God-damned note. I suppose you think it's a big joke!"

"What note?"

"Fuck off!"

"Hold on a minute, Fred. Have you lost your mind? What are you talking about?"

I banged the receiver down. What if he hadn't done it? He'll think I'm a raging lunatic, I thought.

Maybe I am. I looked at the name again. There it was. Matthius, b. Dec 25, 1622.

If it wasn't Dave, then who else? Dave knew I'd been obsessed with the boy. He knew how responsible I'd felt. He knew about Matthew Holbein's delusion that I was his father. It was a sadistic thing to do, and unlike him, but it had to be Brixton.

It was almost seven thirty; I had to go. I put the piece of paper in my inside coat pocket and went home.

Valerie heard my key in the lock and opened the door.

"Happy birthday again, darling!" She put her arms around me and moved her face to kiss me. I drew away, stiffly. She ignored this, took me by the hand, and led me into the living room.

"Happy birthday, Frederic," said Margaret.

"Welcome to middle age," said Alfred.

Lisa moved quickly across the room to hug me. "Happy birthday, Daddy." Jenny joined her.

The Greens were there, too, and the Pattons, two couples Val and I had seen quite a bit of during the past year.

"Happy birthday, F.P., " said Paul Green.

I stood as if mesmerized in the middle of the living room. Their voices seemed dim and far away. I felt as though a lead pipe ran from the base of my skull to the tip of my spine. I looked around the room, from one face to another, feeling that I could barely recognize them. Everything was blurred.

"Hey, fellow," said Alfred. "You can't be that surprised. You look as if you'd seen a ghost."

Everyone laughed.

Except me. Maybe that's just what I was seeing. Or maybe that's what they were looking at and mistaking me for flesh and blood.

Damn Brixton. I'll corner him in the morning and get the truth out of him face to face. The thought yanked me out of my detachment.

"I'm sorry," I said. "It was a surprise, a marvelous surprise. I guess half of me is still back in the office with my last patient—a real problem. I couldn't be more delighted to see you all."

After dinner, I blew out the candles on the devil's food cake with one breath. Everyone applauded.

"Now for the presents," Valerie announced. "Everyone into the living room for coffee and presents."

I opened my presents in a kind of blur, noticing vaguely a new novel by Graham Greene and a gift certificate from Dunhill Tailors.

"One more to go," Valerie said, handing me a large package that, by the shape and weight, had to be a framed picture.

"What is it?" I asked.

"Open it and find out."

As I tore the paper from the frame, a small white envelope fell out. Valerie picked it up and held it while I finished.

"It's an old map," said Lisa. "Look: 1712."

"For your office, darling. You need something to pick the waiting room up, and I thought this was colorful. I found it in Altman's."

I looked at it hurriedly and could make out the quaint geographical impressions of Spain and France and Italy and Germany.

She handed me the note. I opened it. "To my dearest 'Fridericus,' " she had written, "from one who has loved him through all time."

"What the hell is the meaning of this?" I demanded.

She was startled. Everyone was silent.

She began to cry. "My God, Fred, I only wanted to tell you how much I love you." Then her tears turned to temper. "You're behaving abominably."

"Calm down, you two," said Margaret. "I don't know what you're so upset about, Frederic, but I think you're being silly. You owe Valerie an apology."

I sat down, covered my face with my hands for a brief moment, and took a deep breath. "I'm sorry, Val. I don't know what came over me." I looked around the room. Fond as they were of me, only Margaret could conceal her look of complete astonishment. "I apologize to you all." I could feel the paper from Heimwich in my inside pocket, and I knew very well what had come over me, but there was no way I could share this knowledge. How could I say, "Look here, all of you—I may be some kind of specter . . . the rest of you may be real . . . or then again you may not be real either"?

"Poor chap has lost his wits," Paul Green would say.

"Better call the men in the white coats," Bill Patton would suggest.

"I told you psychiatrists are crazy," Harriet Patton would whisper to her husband.

When everyone had left, I began helping Valerie pick up the empty glasses and take them into the kitchen and crumple up the wrapping paper for the incinerator. Neither of us said a word.

At last, as she stood in the hallway, her hand on

the light switch, she asked, "Are you ready for bed?"

I walked over to her and put my hands on her shoulders. "I'm terribly sorry about my behavior, Val. Please
. . . it was a wonderful birthday."

"It was awful," she replied flatly.

"Please forgive me."

"There's nothing to forgive."

I reached to kiss her, but she drew her face away. "Not now."

"Why?"

"I don't want to talk about it."

"Why?"

"I'm terrified, that's why. I thought it was all behind you. Everything's been going along so well. I never would have done it if I hadn't thought by this time you'd simply appreciate . . . oh, God. To see you like this again, only worse than ever—it frightens me. Maybe it will all be fine in the morning."

By the time I came upstairs to the bedroom, less than ten minutes later, Valerie was sound asleep. I undressed in the dark and got into bed and pulled the covers up around me. I felt unnaturally cold.

My mind was racing with memories. Of my mother, coming home on a cold afternoon after shopping, and of myself meeting her at the door and feeling the coldness of her hands on my face. I must have been three or four. The white-brick house we lived in, and my room with the pattern of horsemen and carriages, scenes from boys' adventure stories repeated again and again on the wallpaper, and the window that looked out on the wide lawn that led down to the rose garden my father loved and cared for so well. Walking through the woods with my father on crisp fall days, each of us carrying a walking stick. I must have been around ten. Riding my red bike and ice-skating on the pond and playing hide-and-seek. And later, winning the Latin prize in school and working on the yearbook and the senior dance.

There were scrapbooks and snapshots and home movies to prove that it had all happened. In Morristown, New Jersey, in the United States of America, in the middle of the twentieth century.

I was shaking uncontrollably.

I've never been so cold, I thought. I put on an extra blanket and my winter bathrobe and a pair of socks, but nothing I did could make me feel warm.

~ 11 ~

AT TWO THIRTY I WAS STILL AWAKE. IT HAD BEGUN TO RAIN lightly, and I could hear the rain tapping on the air conditioner that overhung the window. It was pointless just to lie there, but I felt too exhausted and too cold to do anything else. Valerie was sleeping fretfully.

Suddenly I heard a noise, like a door closing and a latch clicking downstairs. It must be from another apartment, I thought. But then there was a louder sound, like a table being moved or turned over, as if someone had inadvertently walked into it in the dark. Impossible, I thought. We're eight stories up and the front door is double-locked and there's no one else here. I got out of bed and walked softly out of the room to the head of the stairs.

At first I could hear and see nothing—then there was a loud crash from the dining room and the clatter and smashing noise of china breaking. My first impulse was to go back into the bedroom, wake Valerie up, and call the police. But then, I thought, suppose there was no one downstairs after I claimed someone was? Considering my behavior earlier in the evening, everyone would be convinced that I was out of my mind. So, instead, I slowly went on down the staircase, halfway, to the point at which I could see, vaguely in the dark, the silhouettes of the furniture in the living room.

Nothing. I went farther down, to the last step, paused a moment, and then flipped on the hall light. I entered the living room first. One of the side tables next to a large wing chair was overturned. A half-dozen books from the bookcases that lined one wall had fallen from the shelf and were scattered on the floor, as if someone had been rifling them in search of something. Valerie sometimes would hide a hundred dollars or more inside a book. It must be a common habit, and burglars probably know all about it. But nothing else had been touched.

I was momentarily frightened. If there were someone there, he might be crouching in the dining room or the kitchen, waiting. So I went back to the hallway and checked the front door. The lock was firmly in place.

Clumsy of me, I thought—I should have checked that out first thing.

I walked briskly into the dining room and turned on the light. A heavy breakfront had fallen forward, striking the dining-room table and remaining propped on it at a crazy angle. China and bric-a-brac were strewn and broken in every direction on the floor.

My God, I thought, we've had a minor earth tremor. Friends in California had described earthquakes, but who had ever heard of one in New York?

As I began to pick up the fragments, sorting out the ones that were permanently damaged from those that looked salvageable, I felt a cold gust of wind across my back, growing louder and stronger as I stood there. I could hear the rain coming down, harder and harder, in a torrential downpour, slamming against the windows. But one of them must be open. Quickly I went back into the living room. The curtains were open. The wind was howling through the room. The rug at the far end of the room was drenched, although none of the windows that lined the wall facing the East River had been left open. All of them had been smashed, and the rain and wind were raging in, unobstructed except by a few pieces of jagged glass that had remained in place. I pulled at the curtains to try to cut down on the damage, but the force of the storm was much too strong, and one whole end was ripped brutally from its fixtures.

Surely Valerie is awake. And the children. I'd better go up and get them. No, I thought, this thing is out of hand. I'd better get the night elevator man instead, right away, and have him wake the super. That is, if he isn't already awake—the whole building must be a madhouse at this point.

Leaving the front door open so that Valerie could see me in the corridor if she came downstairs, I rang for the elevator. It did not come. I rang again, this time keeping my finger on the buzzer. No response.

I'll go down the stairs. That won't take me more than a few minutes. We'll take the elevator back.

I started down the stairs, moving quickly, two steps at a time, holding onto the railing. Suddenly, at the fourth floor, I nearly slipped. The landing seemed to be giving way under my weight. I held onto the railing tightly and stepped backward onto the steps. My other hand, reaching out for more support, touched the wall. It was damp, and the plaster felt soft under my fingers.

Whatever had happened had ripped the entire building apart. I turned to go back to Valerie so we could phone for help. But as I did so, a large section of the stairway leading back to the fifth floor began to sag and then suddenly collapsed.

This thing, whatever it was, was still going on. My God, I should never have left the apartment.

Looking down again, I could see that the door to the fourth-floor corridor was open. I could easily leap across the landing. Then I could get into the hall and try the other stairway in the back of the building.

Why is the place so deserted? I wondered. Why isn't everyone out here, trying to do something? Suddenly I thought of ringing one of the doorbells. Why hadn't I thought of that before? I'll go in and use the phone and can call Valerie and the police from there. I chose the first apartment I reached. There was no answer. I pushed against the door. It opened. What I saw was appalling.

In the light of small fires still burning in scattered heaps, I saw nothing but debris. Scorched walls, broken and burnt fragments of furniture, ashes, as if a flash fire had swept through the apartment in a matter of seconds. Halfway up the stairs, crouched in a position that suggested an effort to escape and then a final and futile attempt to cover herself from the flames, was the dead body of a woman. She was burned beyond recognition. What was left of her face spoke mutely of terrible shock and pain.

I had to find a telephone.

I tried to figure out where she would have placed her phone. As I moved carefully toward the living room, I saw a phone on a small pile of wood and ashes that must have been a table. It had been torn from its wall socket. I froze with shock. The receiver, a foot or so from the wall, was still being gripped by a hand that had been severed from a body that lay on the floor, only a few inches away. The body was covered with dried blood and ashes and twisted into a grotesque position, as if it had been crushed by an overpowering force and left to burn.

I turned and rushed out of the apartment, heading for the back stairs. I wanted to get to Valerie, but looking upward I could see that the stairs were a mass of bent steel wrenched from their supports. Going down, however, they were still intact. If I could reach the street, I could get help.

The lobby was deserted. There was no sign of the night porter. I went outside. It was still raining, but less heavily, and a dense fog had rolled in from the river, so that I could see only a few yards in front of me. The nearest police station was three blocks away. Maybe I would run into rescue squads sooner. Whatever had happened must have affected the whole city. I thought of Valerie and felt sick with helplessness. I ran, as quickly as I could, west on Fiftieth Street toward Second Avenue. The streetlights were out, and the stillness, even at that time of night, seemed unnatural.

I saw a light halfway along the block toward Second Avenue. It glowed and flickered irregularly. The rain had practically stopped now, and someone had lit a bonfire. I ran toward it and saw a group of people huddling around its warmth. As I approached, they covered their faces with their arms.

"What's going on?" I shouted. "What's happened?"

"Get away," one of them snarled.

"Get away," another echoed.

A child was lying on the wet pavement, sobbing.

"What do you mean, get away?" I said firmly. "Where are the police? What's going on?"

An old woman spoke up. "Get away, if you value

your life. We are diseased." Her voice was thin and weak. She coughed, again and again, spitting out blood on the sidewalk. "If you don't want to die, get away."

I wanted to say, "I'm a doctor, I can help you." But momentarily I was halted by the fearful conviction in their voices, and then I thought of Valerie, so I walked on, sometimes running, sometimes slowing down to catch my breath, until I came to the small store on the corner of Third Avenue that usually stayed open all night. It, too, had burned. A man and a woman were sitting on the steps of a nearby brownstone that seemed to have escaped damage. They had a fire going.

"Something to eat?" the man said hoarsely.

"What the hell are you talking about?"

"You'll need something to keep up your strength," he said, without feeling.

"What's going on here?" I asked, desperately.

"This is all we have left," the woman said, lifting the lid from a large wooden container. "When this is gone, there'll be nothing."

I felt like vomiting.

In the dim light of the bonfire, I could see that inside the barrel, in a fluid that combined the smell of vinegar with a horrifying putrid stench, there were what looked like human arms and thighs, covered with muscles, the raw white bones protruding from each end.

This must be some kind of nightmare or hallucination, I thought. This can't be happening. It can't. It's too obscene, too bizarre. I could hear them calling after me as I ran on across Third toward Lexington, toward the police station halfway along that block. No, I had the wrong street. The station was on Fifty-first. I headed up Lexington one block and turned back. Suddenly, the fog lifted; the streetlights were back on again, as if a power failure had been corrected. I could see the modern police station, lighted, intact, and ran as quickly as I could to it.

I went directly to the desk sergeant. "What's been going on?" I asked.

"Power failure. Funny thing for this time of year. But we've got it in hand. They turned the power on again a few minutes ago."

No power failure could account for what I had seen and heard.

"I have to call home."

"Use the pay phone over there."

For a moment I could not recall my home number. I reached for a dime and for the first time realized I was wearing my black dungarees and a sports shirt. I must have dressed before leaving the apartment, though I didn't remember doing so.

I could hear the phone ringing. It was in order—thank God. But there was no answer. I dropped the dime in again and dialed. After four rings, I heard Valerie's voice.

"Are you all right?"

"Of course I'm all right. Where are you?"

I couldn't find the words to tell her. "I'll be there in a few minutes. Don't be afraid. And don't go downstairs."

"Don't go downstairs? What are you talking about?" I could hear a frantic tone in her voice. "What is it, Fred?"

By some stroke of luck, I thought, our apartment has been spared. I hung up and was about to leave the phone booth when a terrible exhaustion swept over me. My legs felt like lead. I could not move them. I felt a strong pressure at the base of my skull and slapped my right palm over the back of my neck. I made one last effort to move, could not, and then sank quickly into unconsciousness.

When I awoke, I was lying in my bed. Valerie was sitting on the edge, next to me. I could see Morton Stein standing behind her.

"What happened?" I asked, and then, "Are you all right, Val? Where are the children?"

"Take it easy, darling," she said. "Of course I'm all right. The children have gone to school."

"You've had a nasty shock," Mort said, softly.

"How did I get here? Did the police bring me home?"

Valerie looked upset. Mort asked, "The police, Fred? Why would they have brought you home?"

"You haven't been anywhere, Fred."

I wanted to protest. I thought of the fire in the apartment below and the people on the sidewalk telling me to get away and the woman opening the top of the barrel and showing me the dismembered human limbs.

"What do you mean, I haven't been anywhere?"

"She means that she woke up around six thirty this morning and went downstairs and found you lying on the floor in the living room, near the windows. You were soaked. You must have gone down to close the windows when it started to rain and collapsed." Mort paused for a moment and then asked, "Did you take anything at bedtime, a sleeping pill or tranquilizer of any kind?"

"No, I don't think so."

"George McLaughlin was in earlier. He checked you over and could find nothing," Mort said.

"Earlier? What time is it?"

"Nearly noon."

"Open the curtains," I asked. It was a bright, clear, sunny morning.

"Do you recall anything else of last night?" Mort went on.

I wasn't about to tell him.

"Valerie said you seemed irritable, upset last evening. Was something troubling you?"

"Nothing really."

"Apparently you didn't have much to drink."

"I don't recall." Wait until I get my hands on Dave Brixton, I thought. "Where's the note?" I asked.

"What note?" Valerie replied.

"A piece of paper, in my inside coat pocket, or maybe I put it on the dresser. Is it there?"

She checked both in a perfunctory way, as if she had not expected to find anything. "No, Fred. What paper are you talking about?"

"Never mind. It doesn't matter."

She handed me a glass of fresh cold orange juice.

"You'd better take a few days off," Mort said. "We've canceled your appointments for today, but I don't think you should go back to work for a few days. Take it easy. I'll come by to see you tomorrow and we can talk. You're in good hands," he added, putting his hand on Valerie's shoulder.

It couldn't have been a dream. It was too real. I wanted to tell them, but not then; maybe later, when I could think about it more clearly . . . I fell asleep.

Mort came back the next day around noon. I was still upstairs. He had obviously decided to use his lunch hour to come by and see me.

"We didn't want to give you all the details yesterday," he said. "Didn't think you could handle them. But you look a lot better today. The fact is that when Valerie went downstairs yesterday morning and found you, the living room was a mess. So was the dining room. You must have been confused, to say the least. Books were strewn around the living room. The breakfront in the dining room had been pushed over onto the table and you'd broken a lot of china."

"It did happen." The statement was involuntary, and Morton picked me up on it right away.

"What happened?" he asked.

I again feigned amnesia. "I mean what you're saying sounds familiar."

"One more thing," he said. "Apparently you burned a bit of paper in the kitchen sink—Val says she'd rinsed out the sink when you and she cleaned up after the party. I wonder why you were burning paper."

I began to feel I could no longer tell what was real and what was not. "Was there a blackout last night?"

"Yes. For an hour or so. You remember that?"

"Vaguely," I replied. "And anything else unusual?"

"Like what?"

"Fire? Damage to the building?" I was being deliberately unclear.

"None that I know of."

Valerie brought Mort a tuna-fish sandwich and a glass of milk. After he had finished eating, he promised to stop by again the next day, and Val showed him downstairs to the door. I could hear them talking in low tones, but I could not make out what they were saying. I could be sure, however, that they felt I was really falling apart.

That was no dream. It happened—as I had blurted

to Mort. And even if it had been a dream, why would I have such a morbid one and why would I go downstairs and do those crazy things that they said I had done? Hallucination? How could that be? No toxic substance. I'm certainly not going to develop schizophrenia at forty-five. And I'm surely not paranoic. Hallucinations can occur in patients with mood disturbances who are depressed, but not unless the depression is really profound, and even then it's quite rare.

But one pattern was holding up. Ever since last September, whenever I had had any contact with the life of Fridericus, it was followed by some turmoil.

Around three, after I reassured Valerie that I would be fine, she went out for an hour to do some shopping. It was noon in California. I dialed Los Angeles information, got the number I wanted, and dialed once more. The voice on the other end had a resonant and almost otherworldly quality to it.

"Rheinhart here."

~ 12 ~

I DID NOT TELL RHEINHART IN ANY DETAIL WHY I WANTED to meet him. But he could easily sense, from the directness of my request and the tone of urgency I used, that the reason was personal and that the earliest possible time was not nearly soon enough.

"I have to be in Washington for a conference on April twenty-fourth. That's less than two weeks from now. Could you fly down on the shuttle and meet me there?"

In my frame of mind I would have taken the first jet to California, but I realized that not only was that impractical; it would have roused Valerie's apprehension, and no doubt I would have met with stiff opposition from Mort. This way, I wouldn't even have to tell them what I was going to do. I agreed to meet him there.

Rheinhart was lecturing at Georgetown. It was one of those clear, delicate early spring days, and as I wandered along Wisconsin Avenue, absentmindedly glancing in the shop windows, waiting to meet him at precisely noon in front of the Georgetown Inn, the purpose of my visit seemed remote and more than a bit foolish. I had returned to work a few days after my strange experience, which, I grew increasingly convinced, must have been a nightmare that caused me to sleepwalk. There had been no further disturbing episodes. I could not find the Xeroxed page with the note that Heimwich had written—or Brixton had simulated—and I had even begun to think that the note had been part of my nightmare, that there might never have been a note on that piece of paper I apparently burned in the kitchen sink.

Rheinhart walked toward me with a vigorous stride, looking taller and younger, despite his gray hair, than I had remembered him from the weekend at Margaret's. He was wearing a blue blazer and khaki twill slacks, and looked more like a member of a country-club executive committee than an expert in the occult. He reached out for my hand.

"Good to see you, Frederic," he said warmly.

"Nice to see you again, Adam. I appreciate your taking the time to meet me."

"Nonsense. It's always a pleasure when one of my establishment-type colleagues decides he wants to find out more about what I am doing. I assume that's why you called."

It was a deliberately leading statement. He knew perfectly well this was not a dispassionate scientific encounter and that my reason for arranging to meet was somehow highly personal.

"Could we find a place to have lunch?" I asked.

"I've already taken the liberty of making a reservation. A little French place called Jour et Nuit, just around the corner a block or two. If that's all right with you?"

In making his reservation, he had obviously specified a table that would afford us considerable privacy, in the very end corner next to an outdoor garden where they would be serving in a month or so. We placed our orders, including half a carafe of house white wine.

Rheinhart leaned back and said, "Well, now. What is this about?"

"I don't know where to begin. As a matter of fact, frankly, it's a little embarrassing."

He sat there, offering no encouragement, waiting.

"The truth is I've been having a difficult period the last year that just doesn't make any sense." I paused. What was I going to say to him? That I thought I might be having a nervous breakdown but I just wanted to check out the possibility of some supernatural influence first? That I'm beginning to think I may be reincarnated and that either the thought of it or the fact of it has been shattering my life? I decided to be simple and straightforward.

I plunged into the episode that had occurred the night of my birthday, for the first time telling anyone the horrifying details. He listened carefully, without comment. As I described waking up in the bedroom with Val and Mort Stein there and what they said about my apparent behavior of the night before, Rheinhart interrupted.

"Could be a dream. You know the dreamer often doesn't recall falling asleep, and if it had not been so detailed and so terrifying you probably would not even question the nature of the experience." Again, it was a leading statement, to get me to be more open in telling him why I thought it might be something other than a dream.

"It could be. But then how do you explain the fact that I included the power failure in it, something that really happened—or that Valerie found me downstairs—or my peculiar—not to say wild—behavior? That breakfront I'm supposed to have pushed over must weigh a ton."

"People do walk in their sleep, and if they are disturbed about something, they can do certain things such as the ones you say Valerie described, even things requiring superhuman strength."

He was beginning to sound like Mort Stein. But why not? He was a psychiatrist, after all, and not an exorcist. "Sure, it could be a dream," I repeated. "It could also be a hallucination, hypnagogic, the kind you can have in that twilight state of being half awake and half asleep."

He smiled. "You don't have to define hypnagogic for me, Frederic. I went to medical school too. As a matter of fact, one of my first articles was on the subject of altered consciousness. Frankly, it sounds too complex for a hypnagogic experience as such."

"Well, what else could it be?"

"I don't know. I don't have enough facts yet. Was there anything in particular that may have triggered your disturbed state that night?"

I was about to tell him about the note—real or imagined—with the names of Pleiert's children on it, involving the coincidence that Matthius Pleiert and Matthew Holbein had had the same birthday. But something inside me balked, and I gave in to a strong impulse to hold back, to stay in control. "Nothing I can think of."

Rheinhart sat there, silently, for a moment. Then he tasted his veal. "Food's pretty good here."

I agreed.

He took a sip of wine. "Tell me, did you ever do anything about following up that curious piece of work by your ancestor—or whatever he was?"

I was startled. "It's incredible," I said, "but I've just realized that I haven't yet told you any of the information I had received on Fridericus." I had omitted all of it, not only that last Matthew-Matthius detail which had so preoccupied me.

I quickly related the few facts I had obtained from Worms and Mulhouse and the results of the search into my own family background, and I added some of the grim picture my reading had given me of life in seventeenth-century Germany.

"Each time I come up with some new piece of information, however harmless it may seem to be, I end up in some kind of emotional turmoil." I then recalled and told him the dream I had had about being part of a painting after he had himself suggested I look for a portrait of Fridericus.

"Are you normally very suggestible?" he asked.

"Quite the opposite."

"And you've been under no other particular strain recently?"

I thought again about Matthew Holbein. "Nothing. Nothing that Mort Stein hasn't helped me figure out." Mort had done that by reminding me that with Caroline's death I had also lost a son. It was a highly personal thing, and I still saw no point in telling Rheinhart. I was only there to find out whether he had any explanation for my terrifying experience.

"Mort Stein. He's a fine psychiatrist. I haven't seen him in years. He was one of my supervisors when I was a resident at Johns Hopkins. I'd have to have considerable respect for what Mort thinks. Of course, he can only look at this experience of yours from the point of view of his own knowledge. But he's sharp."

"He told me to drop the matter entirely. I did. In fact, I had no intention of looking into it any further until that nightmare hit me. Things were getting a lot better."

"It's not like you, though—I'm quite familiar with

your research, as you know, and your other writings—to leave a line of investigation when it is still so thinly tracked."

"I told you. Mort said leave it alone." I felt slightly annoyed and defensive. There was a silence, and I could tell his mind was working at several levels simultaneously. He was sifting what I was telling him through a memory bank of information and experience and constructing and dismissing and reconstructing hypotheses quietly in a fraction of a second.

"Let's see. Heimwich gave you the document in September. Since then you've had a number of episodes of some kind of emotional distress, apparently linked to learning about this fellow Fridericus. Were there any unusual experiences immediately before your trip to Basel?"

I thought a moment. "Nothing I can recall."

"Think harder. It's important."

Yes, Basel was in September. In August we were in East Hampton. "There was the ridiculous experience with a young fortune-teller in East Hampton, at the village fair. She kind of got to me briefly." Until that moment, I had completely forgotten the incident.

Rheinhart leaned forward suddenly. "What was that about?"

I told him simply how she had predicted dire things for me.

"What things?"

"I don't remember." I felt a growing impatience.

"I must know, word by word, if possible, what she said," he insisted.

"This is absurd. I don't believe in fortune-tellers."

"Neither do I, Frederic! But I must know, as best you can recall, exactly what she said."

However compassionate his voice, he was not about

to take a no for an answer. Or "I can't remember."

"Something about fire"—again I thought of my nightmare—"and people dying and me wanting to help but unable to."

"Is that all?" It was as if he knew there must be more.

Of course I remembered her statement that my "son" was in trouble. I'd been upset about Matthew Holbein and she had caught me off guard. Again I resolved not to mention Matthew and went on, "She said my life as I know it now would disappear." Then, I added, slightly sarcastically, "But of course I'd emerge in better shape than before."

"Did she say 'in better shape'?"

"How do I know?"

"What did she actually say?"

"Something about 'real,' or 'genuine.' I can't be sure."

Something I had said pleased him. He sat back in his chair appearing more relaxed, though no less concerned.

"Aren't you going to tell me what you're driving at?"

"Not yet. Not until I have a better sense of the facts. You know better than to ask a doctor to give you his diagnosis and outlook before he's completed his tests," he added, lightly. And then, "Anything else?"

"Peculiar, you mean?"

"Anything. Family. Work. Valerie. Patients. Anything."

"We've just about covered it all."

We had covered nearly everything that had happened over the past eight months. Hearing it all pulled together this way made me feel strange, anxious on the one hand and on the other as though I were watching a second-rate mystery thriller on the "Late Show," with Vincent Price as Adam Rheinhart and some unknown actor playing me.

"Coffee?" the waiter asked. We both nodded.

"There isn't much to go on at the moment, Frederic," Rheinhart said. "However, I can't agree with Stein about just forgetting it. It's gone too far for that."

"You think there's something more to this than what Mort called a focus for some kind of obsessive anxiety? More than a series of psychological reactions in someone who, for some reason, is just plain vulnerable at this time of his life?" It was my way of telling him what I thought, or at least what I hoped it might be. But it was an opinion topped off with a question mark.

"Frankly, yes."

"Spell it out, Adam."

"It is oversimplification of what reincarnation may consist of," he began slowly, "that has made it seem fraudulent or laughable. The laws that govern it and the forms it may take are as complex as any other biological phenomenon. Look at what has happened to theories of matter. Modern physics has dispelled age-old notions about time and space and raised a thousand new unanswered questions. We're barely beginning to understand some of these complexities, and my hope is that with more understanding we'll find better terms to describe what we now quite naïvely call reincarnation. Obviously the possibility that there may be more than a coincidental or even a familial connection to the seventeenth-century Pleiert has begun to reach you, or you wouldn't be here. You know that I consider reincarnation a very real possibility. Much of my

127

work over the last ten years has been an effort to try to demonstrate that objectively."

"I could be running away from facing the fact that I'm falling apart emotionally," I said rather insistently.

"You could be. But I sincerely doubt it. You have too much insight for that. Besides, in my opinion, what you have been going through doesn't fit into any obvious nervous or mental condition."

"There could always be a first time."

"Just listen." He paused, and then added, "I think you may be in a great deal of danger."

"Go on."

"As I said, reincarnation is a very complicated and diverse phenomenon. So are all of the experiences loosely categorized as the parapsychological. Some of the reports are frankly sham. Some may be quite valid. That young fortune-teller who predicted such dire things for you, for example. How did she tell you—did she dramatize it, did she seem to be taking it seriously, or was she indifferent?"

"She was extremely upset, as a matter of fact. She told me tearfully she wasn't very experienced. She had obviously had something happen she didn't know how to handle."

"A critical point. She must have had a genuine vision of something—something out of the ordinary and quite inappropriate for the context in which she was working. Or at least, to her it was genuine. So we are probably not dealing with a hoax. I have seen people who seem to be exquisitely sensitive, able to pick up information— past, present, even what seems to be future—about some- one while in contact with that person. It may seem irra- tional, but that information is valid or subsequently proves to be valid."

128

I was still listening on a different wavelength, thinking of some of those headlines about psychic predictions
in the *National Enquirer*, which would catch my eye occasionally in the A&P while I waited for Valerie to pass through
the checker's line.

Rheinhart must have sensed my continuing skepticism. "Try to keep an open mind, Frederic. I've told you,
we may be involved in a situation of considerable risk.
Let me go on. Our understanding of these phenomena
is practically nonexistent. But that they do occur is beyond
dispute. I think the young woman at the fair must have
had that kind of gift and that she might well have detected
something within you that provoked the mental images
which so startled her she told them to you in that emotional
manner."

He glanced at his watch. "I only have another fifteen
minutes and I want to get to my point, Frederic. Just listen.
And consider. I have no doubt that as our knowledge of
the parapsychological increases, it will seem no more mysterious than radio or television would have seemed to old
Fridericus Pleiert. But right now, we know very little. We
have years, perhaps decades of work to do yet. We need
a few major breakthroughs, a Newton or an Einstein, to
give us new leads to follow. Meanwhile, we are groping
in the dark."

He went on, seriously. "But the fact that we do
not know does not mean it cannot be. There is much evidence, and a lot of it is impressive, though not acceptable
as proof. And those who are collecting it do not always
agree on the value of the evidence they have. We don't
know enough of the processes involved. Personally, I am
presupposing life after death, and that means a surviving
spirit—personality, entity—whatever you want to call it.

129

Will it reincarnate inevitably? Or only sometimes? And if so, why? Have all of us lived before, or are some of us newly incarnated, rather than reincarnated?"

He spoke quietly, intentionally muting his excitement. "The idea of the spirit went out with the emergence of rationality. And like every new trend, the shift from a priori thinking to the experimental and scientific method did not stop at a balanced position. Instead, as always, it moved to an extreme, so that now most of us, particularly in science, are quite convinced that whatever cannot be measured and duplicated in a laboratory simply does not exist."

"What you're trying to tell me, Adam, is that you think that what I've been going through these months adds up to a strong argument for Fridericus and me being one and the same person?"

"For the first time, I detect a note of sincerity in that question, Frederic."

"I am sincere. But if reincarnation is a common thing, as I believe you are suggesting, why would thinking so, or finding it out to some degree, be such a devastating experience, other than the fact that it might go against certain premises the individual already holds?"

"You know as well as I that giving up one set of assumptions in favor of another is a disturbing process, Frederic."

"Not like this. I've been wrong before and have had to change my thinking. But it's never been like this."

"Exactly. That's why I believe we are dealing with something quite complex and potentially dangerous."

"What do you mean?"

"I do not fully know. A great many people assume that reincarnation is a reality, but it does not distress them.

They don't remember previous lives; they just assume them. To some it explains suffering, as expiation for some transgression in a past life—that's karma, of course. Or they can merely speculate comfortably on what or who they may have been. More often they glamorize a past life in their imaginations. But there is no real contact, except, of course, sometimes during early childhood, after which there is complete repression of the residues."

"The normal process, in other words, includes a total forgetting of one's previous existence."

"So it seems. Except in early childhood, as Henderson suggests, and possibly under the influence of hypnosis. But we really don't know."

"Why not hypnotize me, then, and get to the root of this thing now?"

"No," Rheinhart stated firmly, "not hypnosis, at least not now. That, too, could be a real risk. Something has shifted in your life system, placing you in unusual direct contact with what may have been a previous existence."

"And?"

"Something's gone wrong."

I couldn't tell how much of Rheinhart's interest in my predicament was in the opportunity to use it as an experiment and how much was a genuine concern for me.

"I'm going to advise you to do exactly the opposite of what Mort Stein suggested. Rather than trying to leave it alone—I think things have gone much too far for that—I think you must actively search for anything and everything that will clarify the nature of any possible relationship between you and Pleiert. And I don't think you should try to do this through intermediaries. You must do this yourself. Go to Europe. Go to the places where you know Fridericus had been—Worms, Mulhouse, Heidelberg, Basel,

131

Strasbourg. See the original records for yourself. Stand where he stood. Walk about the old sections of the cities and try with an open mind—and this may be hard for you—to pick up any kind of sense of familiarity that may help put you in touch with his times. If you can, find out where he lived, the actual house and street. See if there are any threads that connect to your own life now. The church he must have worshiped in—you said he had often been godfather—the hospital he must have worked in, if it is still there—" He paused. "Find his grave."

"I find this," I said slowly, "rather frightening."

"That's why you must go."

"How can I explain it to Valerie?"

"It's best if she not go with you. Her influence is obviously too powerful a restraint in your present life. Besides, it could be very upsetting for her."

"But she'll put up quite a protest. I'm sure she'll think it's just a further progression of what she thinks is mental fatigue."

"Frankly, I wouldn't tell her."

"I'm not good at lying."

"In this instance, you'll be doing her a great kindness."

"And in two or three weeks, what could I possibly dig up? I wouldn't know where to start."

"I'd assumed that. There's a young man in Tübingen whom I've met a couple of times and with whom I carry on a regular correspondence. Wilhelm Gutheim. Quite bright. Has his Ph.D. in psychology but has been primarily involved in parapsychologic investigations. He's evolved some interesting theoretical points of view about reincarnation. I can arrange for you to meet him. I have no doubt that he would be most enthusiastic about going with you."

"I don't speak German."

"Willy speaks fluent English. He can serve as an interpreter wherever you might need one."

We walked back to the Georgetown campus together, stopping at the main gate to say good-bye.

"And be sure to take accurate notes or tape-record your observations," Adam Rheinhart said, almost as an afterthought.

For an instant, the whole idea struck me as preposterous.

"You really think this is necessary?" I asked.

"Evidently I haven't made myself entirely clear, Frederic. Perhaps I have tried too hard not to frighten you any more than you're already frightened. 'Necessary' is an understatement. Your very existence may be at stake."

I knew that he had more in mind than he had revealed. I also knew that he evidently had no intention of being any more explicit. As he walked briskly away from me along the brick pathway, I could only stand there wondering what in God's name he meant.

~ 13 ~

SWISSAIR FLIGHT 343 LEFT KENNEDY INTERNATIONAL AIRPORT at 6:30 P.M. on Sunday, April 30, headed for Zurich, and I was aboard. The plan called for me to rent a car at the Zurich airport and drive north to Tübingen, where I would meet Gutheim. This would give me the opportunity to stop briefly in Hechingen, where my great-grandfather had been born, no more than half an hour south of Tübingen. I busied myself on the plane, dozing now and then, reading sections of C. V. Wedgewood's classic *Thirty Years War* and studying the Michelin map of Germany to reassure myself that the distances involved were short, and that the bold yellow lines which promised excellent roads would guarantee my arrival in Hechingen before jet lag hit me with full force.

The BMW 330, four-speed drive, forest green, moved with precision as I crossed the Swiss-German border north of Shaffhausen, near the Rhine falls. I stopped briefly for a cup of coffee and pastry at Donaueschingen, the small village in the Black Forest boasting the source of the Danube, then north again, through small villages and towns that fringed the Black Forest on one side and the Swabian Jura on the other. It was clear, cool, exhilarating. Sections of road would lead through thick stands of tall green pines, then open up onto a rich valley, stretching for miles. In the far distance were the gray and yellow plateaus of the Jura. I reached Hechingen about noon, beginning to feel the exhaustion that signaled the fact that in New York it was just about seven in the morning and I had been traveling all night.

The place was a complete surprise. I had somehow expected a small rural village, sitting at the base of the mountain on top of which perched Hohenzollern Castle. Quite the contrary. The castle was there, all right, in the distance, silhouetted against cloud banks. But the "village" was a thriving, modern town, obviously built up considerably since the end of World War II. The older part was on a small hill surrounded by a stream, probably an offspring of the Neckar. I drove up into the Zentrum, the middle of the city. The old church, surrounded by a cluster of remodeled ancient houses, was straight ahead, at the end of the main street. The green valley fell away in every direction around the town, and for a moment, impressed by its beauty, I could not help wondering why my great-grandfather had left such a beautiful place. But then, even the little knowledge I had of the futile nineteenth-century struggle for freedom in the German states against the remnants of feudalism gave me what I thought might be the answer to that question.

The city hall was closed. I walked a few hundred yards to the church, where, with the few words of German I could pull together, I learned from an elderly cleaning woman where the parish offices were.

"So, you are Herr Doctor Pleier." The woman in charge of church records spoke English rather well. She

135

was the person whom the genealogical search organization had obviously contacted to go through the old parish records for me and trace the baptismal and marriage events of the Pleier family back into the past centuries.

It's eight o'clock in the morning in New York, I thought, fending off drowsiness as we perused the old books in which, carefully and meticulously, the names of men and women long dead had been recorded.

"This is as far back as I could go." She pointed to the name Dominicus, father of Franz Joseph Pleier, born in 1784. "I cannot find any record of the birth of Dominicus."

"What would that mean?" I asked.

"That he came from somewhere else or that he was Protestant and converted to Catholicism. Hechingen is largely Catholic. You do know that most of the people in these villages simply adopted the religion of the ruling family and, of course, in the seventeenth century particularly, an area would change from one religion to another as control of the area changed hands and family fortunes waxed and waned with war and politics."

"Was this town, Hechingen, affected by the Thirty Years War?" I asked. I didn't recall seeing it mentioned in Wedgewood's book.

"Of course. It was occupied by many different forces and destroyed more than once. The high castle was only rebuilt in the nineteenth century."

My image of the times in which Fridericus lived was becoming still clearer. The Reformation was the great significant event of the sixteenth century, with the kingdoms and imperial cities of what was later to become Germany either remaining Catholic or converting to Lutheranism or Calvinism. But while religious feelings were intense and these differences set the stage for the Thirty Years War, the war itself was primarily one of power and real estate. Nor was it really a German war, although that was largely where it was fought.

The great power in Europe at the time was the Hapsburg empire, which, allied with Spain, was strongly Catholic. The emerging power was France, which, although Catholic, saw the Hapsburgs as an obstacle and serious threat to its future. Hence France allied herself with the Protestant rulers in North German provinces and with the Swedes. The event that set off the struggle was the effort of the electors to unseat the Hapsburgs and choose a Protestant emperor. The result was three decades of devastation, largely taking place in southwest and central Germany and along the Rhine, directed from Paris and Vienna and the north. Fridericus was twenty-three years old when it began and, if, as the records indicated, he died in 1640 at the age of forty-five, the war still had eight more years to run its course.

I was six years old when World War II was started. I was twelve when it ended. Had it gone on for thirty years, I would have been nearly forty—if I had survived it at all.

I had stayed in Hechingen longer than I intended, but it took me only a half hour to reach Tübingen. Following directions explicitly, I found Willy Gutheim's house without much difficulty.

"Come in, come in, Dr. Pleier. It is good to meet you." He ushered me into a book-lined room with a wide picture window that looked down on the old town and the river. "You must be tired."

My reset watch said four o'clock; automatically I

figured that in New York it was eleven in the morning.

"Why don't you take a rest, and then we can talk."

When I awoke it was dark. I reached over and turned on a small bedside lamp. For an instant I was unsure of where I was, in a strange room with orange curtains and a large oak armoire. Then the fog cleared. Of course. Tübingen. Gutheim.

I went downstairs. Gutheim offered me a drink.

"Scotch, with a touch of water," I said.

Gutheim asked, "Ice?"

"Of course. All Americans devour ice, you know."

He was a very big man, probably six feet five, with thick blond-brown hair, rugged features, stocky but not fat, looking as though he belonged on the ski slopes at Zermatt or roaring down the Colorado River on a raft. Somewhere in his early thirties. Not at all what I had expected.

"You'll have to forgive the sloppiness of my place. I'm not married—I live alone. My housekeeper has been ill."

"After New York, everything looks clean enough to eat on," I said.

He slumped into a large black-leather chair, stretched his legs out in front of him, swirled his whisky in his glass, and said, "Intriguing—this business that brings you here. Rheinhart told me a bit about it. How is Adam?"

I explained that I hardly knew him.

"You should. You should get to know him better, I mean. He is quite a person. A real pioneer. Of course, I have sometimes become impatient with his plodding persistence in trying to validate everything he does with the scientific method, but I admire him greatly for it."

"I don't understand, Dr. Gutheim."

"There are many ways of arriving at truth. Of course, truth is a relative thing anyway. I suppose I'm more of a theoretician, guided"—he made a sweeping movement of his right hand—"by bursts of intuitive insight. By the way, call me Willy."

After having grown used to the formalities of my psychiatric colleagues in Europe, it was refreshing to deal with Willy Gutheim.

"And I shall call you Friedrich."

"Please."

"I have given much thought to your predicament. Rheinhart tells me you think you may be having some kind of mental aberration, but you still decided to pursue the so-called supernatural possibilities of your situation. Is that right?"

"More or less. Although, frankly, since I spoke with him I've been feeling a good deal better. I'm even wondering what I am doing here, no offense intended."

"No offense heard." He smiled. "But"—he went on, drawing out the word and raising a hand for emphasis—"it is a good thing you did come and that you are willing to look further into this."

"Why do you say that?"

"Partly selfish. I'm always eager to get interesting cases for study." Before I could misunderstand him, he went on, "But primarily because I think, as Rheinhart does, that your life, at least as you know it now, may be at risk."

I was silent, but he read my question from my face.

"Why, I cannot be sure yet. I have only a speculation. I'd rather not prejudice our work by sharing it with you now. And if things work out as I hope and expect they will, I believe we can avert the danger." He stood up and came toward me. "Let me tell you my plan." He added gently, "Then we can go have some supper."

He led me to a large table desk on top of which lay a map of southwest Germany with a number of red circles and connecting lines.

"These are the places we must go. Ideally, I would follow the sequence of Fridericus's life, from Worms, south to Strasbourg, north again to Heidelberg, and so forth, but I do not believe that is necessary. We can approach this in a more convenient way, starting here"—he pointed to Heidelberg—"going then to Worms and on down to Strasbourg, Mulhouse, and finally Basel."

He folded the map up, revealing, underneath, detailed plans of each city in question.

"These are contemporary maps of each place. Of practical use. We are, of course, only interested in those sections which were part of the original cities in the time of Fridericus."

He pushed them aside and, opening a large brown manila folder, said with decided pleasure, "And here are drawings and maps of each city in the late sixteenth or early and mid-seventeenth century. Let me tell you, they were not easy to come by, especially this one of Worms."

He had several maps of each city, drawings in some instances, woodprints in others, black and white only. Each portrayed a city from an aerial view, showing old walls ringing them, church and cathedral spires, and narrow, twisting streets. In the case of Worms, he also had a drawing of the city as seen from the Rhine, with each tower and steeple identified by name.

"I also have pictures of special places sketched around that period." He showed me one of the cathedral in Worms.

"In the morning, I would like you to go over these,

one by one"—there must have been fifty drawings in all—
"carefully, letting your mind wander, noting anything that
looks familiar, any names that stimulate recollection, any
coincidences with your present life that may strike you;
in fact—you are a psychiatrist and understand the process
of association—anything at all that might occur to you."

"Sounds like an inkblot test," I said.

"In a way it is. You see, one of the troubles with
this kind of search is that in many instances the original
buildings have of course been destroyed and new ones
have taken their place."

I thought of Hechingen.

"In Basel that is not as true, or in Strasbourg. But
the other places, Worms especially, could be a problem."

"I only caught a glimpse of Tübingen, driving in
this afternoon. It looks like a beautiful medieval city."

"Tübingen was more fortunate than some of the
others," he said. "Take Heidelberg. At the beginning of
the Thirty Years War it had five thousand inhabitants and
was one of the leading university cities in Europe. By 1650,
there were only five hundred people left. Invasion. Recurrences of the plague. Whatever. And then, in the late part
of the seventeenth century, the French descended on it
and burned much of it to the ground. The Sun King,"
he added ironically. Then: "You must be getting hungry.
Let's eat."

The next morning I did as Gutheim requested. I
spent nearly four hours poring over the old maps and
drawings. At first I was excited about the possibility of
finding some clue, but as item after item failed to evoke
the slightest response in me, my disappointment grew and
then faded to boredom.

"Well?" Gutheim asked, cutting a piece of cheese

and opening a bottle of dark beer for his lunch.

"Nothing."

He did not seem surprised.

"There was one thing," I said, as an afterthought.

"What?" he asked casually.

"The name Peter. I noticed that both Worms and Heidelberg have either a cathedral or a main church named after St. Peter. And in Basel, I recall the Petersgasse in the old part of Basel when I was there in the fall."

"And?" He sounded as if he were quite aware that I was struggling too hard to find connections.

"For a couple of years, in my teens, I went to a private boarding school in the States called St. Peter's."

"Probably artifact," he said, pouring his beer into a tall glass. "But it may be a beginning."

It took us nearly three hours to drive north to Heidelberg the next morning. Willy assured me we could have done it more quickly, but he chose to take a smaller road that followed the Neckar River, by way of Eberbach. Everything was exquisitely pastoral, the houses in each small village trimmed with flower boxes, the air sweet with spring.

By the time we reached the outskirts of Heidelberg, the Rhine was considerably wider, allowing barge traffic. As we entered the city, we had an immediate view of the old town to the south of the river and, dotting the north bank, the large, nineteenth- and twentieth-century homes, looking like miniature palaces. Rising like a fortress above the roofs was the castle.

"It'll be worth taking a trip up to the castle, even though it was thoroughly demolished after Fridericus's time and much of it is still in ruins. But if he was a student here, he might at some point have climbed to it and at least stood outside its walls. He might even have been invited inside."

His last remark revealed his distaste for the social structure of the times. Nobility. Peasants. And in between, the middle class, consisting of shopkeepers, tradesmen, petty politicians, lawyers, university professors, masons, and even doctors. The nobility set the stage for events on a grand scale, and everyone else paid the price.

We parked the car and started to walk.

"Just the old sections," he reminded me. "And make note of whatever you experience as we go about."

We went to the place where the old university had been and the place where the old hospital had been, past shop after shop of souvenirs, a few interesting antique stores. I stopped near a small street with what appeared to be old houses in it.

"Not here," he said, brusquely. "Eighteenth century. Let's keep moving."

I was astonished to see, on the main street, one of Uncle Alfred's hamburger stands. "They're almost as popular here as sausage," Willy remarked.

We reached St. Peter's Church. Each of the stone carvings stationed irregularly along the outside walls attested to a noble or wealthy family buried nearby. We tried to go inside, but it was locked. Willy translated a sign telling us it was closed for repairs.

"Damn," he muttered. "Let's try the Holy Ghost Church."

"Built in the early fifteenth century," he commented as we entered, stopping at the historical plaque. "Gothic," he added. "Supposed to be the largest in the Palatine."

Over the years I had seen plenty of cathedrals in

France and England, all Gothic, but the simple lines of the Holy Ghost, diminutive by comparison, struck me as particularly peaceful. I shared my thought with Willy.

"Nothing peaceful about this place," he said. "In 1692 or 1693, thereabouts, the French raped the place and tore the bodies of the electors, the rulers, out of their coffins and threw them in the streets and took the coffins with them as loot."

"Nothing here," I said. "It's impressive, but no déjà vu."

"All right. Let's go to the Haus zum Ritter."

Now a hotel, the Ritter House had been built in 1592 by a fugitive Huguenot, Charles Belier. Its highly decorated exterior and the way in which the facade curled to peak at the top of the roof struck me as decidedly Dutch. We had a delicious lunch there, but it was uninterrupted by any "vibes."

We took a cable car to the castle.

"As I said, it's worth a look. And you may find the pharmaceutical museum interesting."

It was. Room after room contained herbal compounds and medicines, ancient recipes and utensils and a model of the typical chemist's laboratory of the sixteenth and seventeenth centuries. I could easily envision Fridericus standing over an oven, waiting for some powdery substance to heat to the desired temperature, grinding roots and petals in a clay bowl to prepare a drug to help some patient find relief from terrible intestinal pains.

Still nothing.

As we drove the short distance, less than an hour, to Worms, on the other side of the Rhine, the beautiful countryside gave way to large chemical factories and endless rows of smokestacks.

Mannheim and Ludwigshafen. They did not even exist in Fridericus's times. For me they were names from news broadcasts on the old Fada radio about allied bombing raids when I was ten.

For the first time we saw a signpost for Worms.

"It can't be too important a city," I remarked, thinking I was passing judgment on the German highway-sign system.

"It isn't," said Willy, "except that this is good wine-growing country. Historically, the last important event to happen here was probably the Diet of Worms in the sixteenth century which produced the edict denouncing Martin Luther. The twelfth-century cathedral is considered very beautiful."

I could see the distant spire of what must be the cathedral.

"How did you get into this line of work?" I asked Willy. By now, our first effort to stir up something in me about the past having been a complete failure, I was beginning to feel sorry that I was offering a somewhat sterile project. I also felt greatly relieved.

"It's a complicated story, but I'll try to make it brief. I majored in psychology, and the mysterious always had an irresistible attraction for me. Had I lived centuries ago, I would probably have been a navigator, like the Spanish or English or Portuguese. Discovering new lands. But now, I believe, the unknown continents are either out there in space or in here—" he placed his right forefinger on his forehead.

"And, of course," he went on, "there is always a personal reason. My father died when I was eight. He had survived the war, a lieutenant in Rommel's Afrika Korps, and was killed in 1954 in a motor accident. He was only thirty-five and my mother could not accept his death. She spent what little money she had going to spiritualist mediums so that she and he could 'communicate.' I loved my father very much, but for her to be so obsessed—as though she just lived from one séance to the next—I thought that could not be right. And I grew up ever more certain that those people were faking—were feeding her obsession to get money out of her. By the time she died—when I was twenty-three—I had started looking into parapsychology, determined to get back at the fakers who had robbed my mother of her money and her mind."

I said, surprised, "You went into this just to prove them wrong?"

"That was the primary reason."

"And what kept you interested was the mystery of it?"

"Yes. I did expose a few fakers. But the more I looked into it, the more I realized that there were a great many unopened doors and unanswered questions. I met people like Rheinhart. I knew that I had to go on and make this my life."

It was a strange twist, I thought.

We had entered a residential street. A sign read, MITSTADT, with an arrow pointing to the left, and Willy said, "To the center of town, yes." I shifted the BMW into third and made the turn. A few hundred feet farther on, we passed under the arch of the old city wall. If I had known then what the next two days were going to be like, I would have turned the car around in the middle of the road, headed back to Ludwigshafen, and taken the very first plane out of Germany.

146

~ 14 ~

THE DOM HOTEL WAS ANYTHING BUT A HOTEL IN THE GRAND Europcan manner. We drove around and past it several times before figuring out how to reach the front door. The solution lay in walking into the entrance of the local movie theater and then, instead of buying a ticket and going in to see the film, taking a small elevator next to the box office up one flight to the hotel lobby.

At the Dom, the innkeeper was a pretty young girl of about twenty-five, and the lobby, though small, was comfortable and briskly clean. Willy and I took separate but adjacent rooms. Willy's was just about large enough to accommodate his massive frame.

Ten minutes later we were on the street again, in front of the cinema.

"Where is Worms?" I asked.

"This is it. We'll look at the new part of the city first. Then it will take us about fifteen minutes to walk through the old part, what there is left of it."

I remembered the terse letter from the Worms archives that accompanied the few bits of information I had received about Fridericus. Something about a fire.

147

"What the French didn't finish in the early sixteen hundreds, they did by 1689. And what was left was taken care of by the Allies in 1945," Willy reminded me.

It was one thing to know that. It was another to see it at first hand. I had held onto the image of an old walled city with twisting streets and leaning buildings, clumped tightly together, interrupted every so often by a large plaza and a church. So far, the fragment of the wall and gate that we had passed through was the only evidence of antiquity I had seen. We were in the new part now. It was mostly a city of small-scale glass and aluminum buildings, and looked as if it had sprung up after the war on the fringe of some Florida housing development. There was only a cathedral spire to make the difference, and that was well away from this section.

"Let's do a cursory survey now, while there's still some light. Tomorrow we can spend more time in a few specific places, and go to the archives," Willy said. "We'll start at the Dom Platz," he announced.

We left the street and cut through a well-cared-for public garden, edged by a remnant of old wall, perhaps Roman, and in less than three minutes we were standing in the courtyard of the Cathedral of St. Peter.

I was struck at once by the simplicity of its lines. Four towers, dotted with small windows, more like a fortress than a house of God, rose symmetrically about the neighboring buildings, each crowned with a conical roof. There were no gargoyles, none of the detailed carvings and decorative frills that I recalled seeing in so many French churches. The overall effect was one of sturdiness, though not without grace. "This is twelfth-century Romanesque," Willy said.

We walked along the south side of the building.

"That's the St. Nicholas Chapel," Willy remarked. "Just beyond it is the south portal, the one used to get into the cathedral."

The door was locked. Above and to the right was a carving of the cross keys of the fisherman saint. I wondered if Fridericus had walked through these doors and gone into the church, and knelt and prayed, three and a half centuries ago. Perhaps, but I couldn't even be sure of his religion. He might have been Catholic or Lutheran, a Calvinist, or even an agnostic.

With Willy leading the way, we crossed a main street to the south of the Dom Platz called Andreasstrasse. As we did, a wave of excitement rushed through me and a peculiar sense of familiarity.

He pointed to a small, enchanting church, single-spired, that lay directly in our path, in the center of another square.

"St. Magnus," he said. "It's one of the oldest Lutheran churches in Germany. Completely destroyed. That's a restoration on the original site, after the Second World War."

I was disappointed. "I was just about to tell you I finally felt something," I said, "and now you tell me it's only about twenty years old."

He did not react, but merely moved forward toward a building which was obviously very old, beyond which stood more of the old city wall and a gate with a sentry tower.

"This is the Andreasstift. Restored, but still largely authentic. Dates back to the thirteenth century. And the old gate is original. That's the city museum. We'll go there in the morning," Willy stated.

Twilight was casting a gray haze over the city. It

149

was beginning to drizzle. Streetlamps began to glow with small halos in the mist.

"Let's just swing around to the right, here, and walk back to the hotel, past the Jewish cemetery," he suggested.

A thousand or so ancient tombstones stood irregularly behind a high wall, some leaning precariously, others elevated where the ground formed small mounds. Even in the dim light, it was possible to see the Hebraic lettering on a few of the stones closer to the road.

"Worms was kind to the Jews, at times. A refuge for them. There was quite a thriving Jewish community here in the Middle Ages," Willy said. "During the Nazi regime, the people in Worms concealed the cemetery from the government, though I don't know how they did it. Otherwise it would have been destroyed."

There was a chill in the air.

"Let's head back to the Dom," I said. "I'm getting cold—and hungry."

Willy decided that he would rather take a bath, have a drink, and go to bed early than go out to eat. I quickly discovered that there was no room service at the Dom and decided to go downstairs to the hotel restaurant for a bite. It was half-past seven—two thirty in the afternoon in New York, and I might catch Valerie at home.

The girl behind the desk was not only pretty, she was very pleasant as well.

"I'm sorry, but the dining room is closed for repairs today," she said. "But there are several places I can suggest for you to eat."

"You speak English quite well," I commented.

"I studied in the United States for a year, at the University of Colorado," she said.

"Are you from Worms originally?"

150

"No. From Mannheim. Are you and your friend here on business?" she asked.

"More or less. History." I certainly wasn't about to tell her we were searching for clues to some other life I might have led. I felt foolish enough admitting it to myself. "I wonder if you could place a call for me to the United States, to New York. Is there a phone down here I could use?"

She explained the procedure and motioned to a booth at the other side of the lobby.

"When it rings, pick it up," she said.

I had been to Europe often enough not to feel the sense of dislocation and confused identity that the traveler to a foreign place sometimes feels, the sort of feeling that makes you wonder at times not only where you are and what you are doing there, but that even gives you the slightly euphoric sense of being someone else, free of the problems you had when you boarded the plane at home. There were other places in Europe where I could come and go as easily, from a mental point of view, as going to Boston or Carmel. But the last few days, Tübingen, Hechingen, Heidelberg, and now Worms were somehow different. There was a strangeness about this place that made me feel decidedly a stranger to myself. It had nothing to do with the purpose that Willy and I were engaged in, although that certainly intensified it. I recalled feeling that way in Rome, years before, sitting on the balcony of the Hassler Hotel overlooking the gardens and the city, having breakfast in the bright Italian morning. It was my very first trip to Europe. I'd been away nearly three weeks, and the remoteness of my ordinary life at home had gradually grown so great that I was beginning to feel, not unpleasantly, as if I were another person.

The sound of Valerie's voice instantly brought back my sense of reality. I felt as if I could reach out and touch her.

"Val, darling. You sound as if you were right here, down the street."

"Where are you, Fred?"

"Munich." I hated to tell her that lie.

"How's everything going?"

"Marvelous." I caught myself. I didn't want to seem too enthusiastic. After all, I was supposed to be at a conference on psychopharmacology. "But I miss you," I added quickly.

"I miss you, darling. Are you all right?"

"Fine. How are the children?"

"Lisa got an A in her math exam. Jenny's puttering along. One minor piece of bad news, though. The wall in the bedroom started to peel. The caulking they did last year wasn't good enough, so on top of the winter, we've had some pretty heavy wind and rain the last few days and the water's seeped through."

To most people this would have been a minor annoyance, solved by the superintendent or the managing agent's looking at it and repairing it. For me it only served as a reminder of my frightening experience the night of my birthday and why I was in Worms in the first place. I was totally silent for a moment.

"Is something wrong?" Val suddenly asked.

"No. No. Everything's fine."

"Please. Take it easy, darling. You know you haven't been yourself, and I was never wildly enthusiastic about this trip."

She, too, must have been thinking of the episode, but in an entirely different way.

"Where can I reach you?" she asked.

I lied again. "We're going down to the country to-morrow, to the home of one of the doctors here, for a day or two. It's about an hour and a half from Munich. I don't know the number. I'll have to call you."

"Please, be sure to call me."

"I will."

As I hung up the receiver and glanced briefly at the girl behind the desk, I felt sick. I had an image of Valerie calling Brixton to find out exactly where the conference was being held in Munich and discovering he knew nothing about it. Then she might ask Bernice, who innocently would give her the telephone number of Professor Egelbord in Munich, and Valerie would call his office and his secretary would say he had been away somewhere for several weeks and that she was not familiar with any such meeting. And Valerie would panic, but keeping her wits about her would systematically check, first with the travel agent, then the airlines, and find out that I had flown to Zurich. She would probably get all the way to Avis and they would tell her that a Dr. Pleier had rented a BMW at the Zurich airport. But that would be as far as she would be able to go—to envision me driving off somewhere in a rented car—but where?—and utter helplessness would sweep through her.

My daydream ended there.

"Is anything wrong, sir?" the girl at the desk asked.

"No. Thank you." I was suddenly ravenously hungry. "How do I get to one of those restaurants you mentioned?"

Following her directions, I walked back across the Dom Platz to Andreasstrasse, turned east, and within a hundred feet reached the corner of the main shopping street, Neumarkt. On the far corner of the Dom Platz, on the second floor of a three-story modern office building, a bright-red neon sign flashed on and off through the haze and darkness. China Haus, it said incongruously. This was one place she had suggested, but somehow I could not see myself eating chow mein or Szechwan shrimp in the middle of Germany.

On the near corner was another place, crowded with people. I looked through the window. Wooden tables were covered with red-checked tablecloths and a fat candle sat comfortably in the middle of each table. It seemed pleasant enough. I put on my glasses and studied the menu posted at the door. As I was going down the list of dishes, occasionally sounding them out loud to figure them out, I became uncomfortably aware of two men in black raincoats, standing a few feet away, watching me. I decided to ignore them and go on in. But as my hand reached for the door to push it, one of them called out to me.

"You're an American, aren't you?" The tone was friendly enough.

I turned around and said, "Yes."

"We are too. You gonna eat in there?" His accent seemed as anomalous as the China Haus sign. But it was refreshing.

"We know a better place around the corner," the second, smaller man said. "Better food, and not as expensive. Would you like to go with us?"

"Thanks," I replied, "but this looks fine to me. Are you tourists?"

"No," the first man answered, laughing. "Do we look like tourists?" He went on, "U.S. Army."

I was surprised.

The first man kept on talking. "There's a big base

here. Information center and supplies. In fact, it's one of the town's main industries, or at least it used to be before the dollar started to get into trouble. Now we pretty much stay on base. Can't afford town prices."

An Army base? How did I know it wasn't some kind of con? But I was not interested in either their credentials or their company. I just wanted my dinner.

"Well, thanks for your invitation, but I think I'll go in here," I said. "Good-bye. Nice talking to you."

I went inside, and the waitress showed me to a table. The people around me were talking loudly, drinking beer in big, handsome steins, laughing, cutting away at large portions of meat and black bread. Plenty of local atmosphere, I thought. Looking up from the menu, I suddenly noticed that the two Americans were still standing at the window, peering in. As my eye caught theirs, a large silver cross on the chest of the smaller man reflected the light from the window for a moment, until he pulled his coat around him, and they slowly turned away and disappeared into the night.

The English-speaking waitress helped me order, and, as it turned out, the food was quite good. At last I had found a place that would serve sauerkraut. Willy had warned me, when I told him I was looking forward to the real thing, that there was a sort of national sensitivity about sauerkraut, and it was hard to find except in someone's home. I ordered half a carafe of white Rhine wine. As I sat there, sipping the last of it after I had finished my meal, I felt some of the contagious warmth and relaxed joviality of the people beginning to reach me.

I had brought along my copy of Wedgewood's *Thirty Years War* and read it, on and off, throughout supper. I had reached the defeat of Tilly's forces at Breitenfeld by

King Gustavus of Sweden. The tide of war had turned, for the first time, against the Catholic Emperor Ferdinand. That was Christmas, 1631. The Spanish allies of Ferdinand still occupied the Rhine—and Worms—but their hold of that territory was not to last much longer. The Swedes had turned westward and were heading for the Palatinate.

Fridericus was a physician. I wondered if he had succeeded in staying aloof from the political and religious struggles of his times. I could see him walking the streets of the city on his way to the hospital, caring for the sick regardless of who occupied the city, quietly affirming that the affairs of the world were not his concern, that he was, first and only, a healer.

As I finished paying the check and was putting on my topcoat, I suddenly heard the somber ring of a church bell. I looked at my watch. It was ten. The bell tolled again. Automatically, like someone listening to every detail of a weather report, I began to count the tolling. As I stepped outside, it had rung nine times. One to go.

But the bell did not stop. It kept on: twelve, thirteen, fourteen. And it seemed to be growing louder. Probably hooked up to some timer that's gone out of order, I thought. Nineteen, twenty. My eardrums began to hurt from the noise.

I walked back toward the cathedral. I could hear the sound of other bells from all around the city, ringing again and again, building to a loud and almost deafening crescendo. As I approached the Dom Platz, still concealed behind a row of buildings, I could hear the sound of voices, the low, massive hum of crowds, and I could see the glow of some great light flowing out from where the plaza was located. Then, in the shadows, I saw the figure of a young man, frail and in rags, moving toward me, waving, beckoning me on. Suddenly he turned and ran toward the cathedral. As he did, I caught a glimpse of his profile in the light. My God, I thought. It can't be . . . Matthew Holbein!

I ran quickly after him. The bells were ringing frenziedly, as if they would never stop. I turned the corner. There in front of me, carrying torches, milling about in a confused fashion, were several hundred people in a clotted mass that filled the square around the base of the cathedral. Some were carrying long sticks, some were shouting unintelligibly, others were huddled together—men, women, and small children—looking like shadows in the flickering light of the firebrands. Matthew Holbein, if that was who it had been, had vanished in the crowd.

I stood there, motionless, terrified.

~ 15 ~

THE CROWD HAD ITS PURPOSE, DISORGANIZED AS IT SEEMED.
Pressing on in my direction, toward the Andreasstrasse,
they were led by half a dozen figures, hooded in black,
two of whom had hold of and were dragging with them
an elderly woman. I could barely make out her features.
Her long gray hair hung down over her shoulders. Every
now and then she would become limp and fall toward the
ground, but before she could, the two figures would
brusquely pull her up and yank her forward again. At one
point, she stood still, looked up at the sky, and let out a
terrifying shriek. The voices of the crowd stilled momentarily. Someone ran forward and struck her across the face.
The church bells, which had been steadily ringing, stopped
as if by signal. Then, in a harsh, colorless pattern, like
an old black-and-white film, the throng once again began
moving toward where I was standing.

I turned around quickly. There was the small
church, the square behind it, and beyond that the Andreasstift. I began to run and kept going without looking
back, until I reached the shelter of the building's columns.
The door, which had been locked a few hours before, was

wide open. I ran inside and paused to catch my breath.

I don't understand. How can this be real? What's happening to me?

I looked out hesitantly. Before my eyes, the people had assembled in the plaza, halfway between the cloister and the church. In the center of the open area in front of them was a pile of brushwood and, stretching up into the night, a tall stake. The hooded figures were tying the struggling woman to the pole. Then they stepped back while several of the others used their torches to ignite the branches that lay beneath. She spat at them, cried out again, but her screams were drowned out by the shouting of the crowd. The flames rapidly leaped up around her. For one instant I could see her face, contorted in pain. Then I could not see anything except the vague outline of a twisting body hidden by the blaze.

Suddenly I felt the grip of hands on my upper arms. I pulled away, jerking myself free, and swung about. A large bearded man, his face grossly disfigured with scars and pox, confronted me. His clothes were in shreds, encrusted with dried blood, and emitting a vile stench. He lunged toward me, grabbing my coat and, as I jumped back, tearing it off. I turned and ran out, but there was no way to go except through the crowd or, to my left, through the gate and beyond the city wall.

I could see immediately that the gate was closed. The wall, reaching out in either direction beside it, was intact, and on the ramparts I could make out men in uniforms standing every twenty feet or so, helmeted, some with crossbows, others with flintlocks.

I must be going mad. I've got to find my way back to the hotel and Willy and get some help. But if the thought that what I was experiencing was an illusion was in some strange way comforting, my self-assurance was completely shattered by the sound of muskets firing from the walls.

The crowd began to disperse, with people running frantically in every direction. I ran halfway across the square, behind the place where the remains of the charred woman hung from the post, not daring to look up at her, until I came to a side alley.

If I could find my way back to Neumarkt, I thought futilely, I might be all right. This passageway seemed to lead in the right general direction. It was deserted. Slowing my pace to avoid being observed, I walked along the narrow street for a hundred feet or so. Another hundred feet away, straight ahead, I could see lights. It had to be Neumarkt and the neon signs of the shops. I moved on more quickly, but as I did the lights seemed to fade and take on the irregular, flickering glow of fire. Suddenly I heard a loud whirring noise in the air above my head, and just as suddenly a loud crash. The wall of the house just ahead of me to the right crumbled. Debris fell into the alley, and the building burst into flame.

I could hear the steady pounding of cannon in the distance. I had never heard the sound before, but its thundering quality was unmistakable.

"Friedrich. Friedrich."

Someone had recognized me. It must be Willy, there in the darkness, hidden by smoke. No, not big like Willy. A smallish priest, in a long black cassock, with a crucifix around his·neck. He took my hand.

"*Kommen mit mir,*" he said firmly. I felt compelled to go with him, to leave my hand in his. He pulled me back along the alley to the square, never letting go of me, toward the cathedral. Hundreds of people were swarming onto the Dom Platz, pressing toward the south portal

160

of St. Peter's, pushing one another aside in their haste to get through the doors and into the church. If he was trying to take us there, I thought, we would never make it through that mob.

Seemingly out of nowhere a dozen or more men on horseback, swords in hand, appeared among the churning crowd, raising their arms and thrusting them down again and again, with vicious determination. The night resounded with agonizing screams.

"Blutdürstig Franzüsen!" the priest whispered in suppressed fury. Then he tightened his grip on my hand, pulling us toward the north side of the building, beyond the St. Nicholas Chapel and into the gardens that Willy and I had walked through that same afternoon. He led me to a small wooden door in the Roman wall, hidden by shrubs, and opened it slowly and with great effort. Reaching inside, he grabbed a lighted torch off the wall, drew me through the doorway, and closed the door behind us. For the first time, he let go his hold on me and stepped in front, beckoning me to follow him down a narrow stairway, damp and musty, that obviously ran to a passage under the ground.

"Mach schnell!" he urged.

At the bottom of the steps was a tunnel, about four feet wide and less than six feet high. I had to stoop to enter it. The walls were damp. In the light of his torch, the shadow of a large rat, grotesquely exaggerated, scurried across the wall.

"Mach schnell!" he repeated.

The tunnel ran in a straight line before us, illuminated only as we moved forward. I was hunched over, shuffling, following the small form of the priest, nearly choking on stale and fetid air. It could not have taken more than five minutes to get through the tunnel, but it seemed like hours. At the end, it opened into a large crypt, already lit with candles, in which thirty or so people huddled around the stone coffins of long-dead noblemen and bishops. We were underneath the cathedral.

A young woman dressed in black moved toward me. Her features were delicate, her eyes sad. She looked at me silently, then embraced me.

"Friedrich. *Gott sei Dank!*" whispered a tall, gray-bearded man who reached his hand out and put it tightly on my shoulder.

These people seemed to know me. They do know me.

I know them.

Until that moment, everything had been fuzzy, as if I had been looking through the unfocused lens of a camera. But suddenly, as if the lens had been brought into focus, shapes and colors took on vivid definition.

A long way off, I could hear the regular sound of the guns, roaring rhythmically like the roll of a drum.

The young woman had returned to a matting of straw at the far end of the crypt. Two small children sat next to her. I walked over to them and reached out for her hand.

"Anna Katherine," I said slowly.

~ 16 ~

IT WAS DARK AND BITTERLY COLD. THE GROUND WAS COVERED
with snow. I was crouching next to a low wall, partly covered by branches, hiding, numb with fear. I could hear
voices, speaking in French, on the other side of the wall.
The lights of their lanterns swung back and forth.

Someone calling my name.

"Pleier! Pleier! Where are you?"

My God, I thought. They've found me!

"Pleier." The voice was insistent.

Then a light, shining directly in my face. The tall
frame of a man standing over me. I shielded my head
with my arms, waiting for the sharp, cutting jab of steel
or the tight grip of hands pulling me from the ground,
deliberately twisting and breaking my arms.

"Friedrich. Thank God. I thought I'd lost you!"

Willy Gutheim was kneeling beside me, touching
me gently on the shoulder. I lost consciousness.

I opened my eyes and looked around. I was lying
in a large bed, covered with a thick, soft, yellow comforter.
The sun was streaming through a window, partly hidden

by a half-drawn shade. A green armchair stood in one corner of the room, a standing lamp next to it. Against the far wall I could see a tall armoire of dark wood. Suddenly I knew where I was, but not how I got there. It was the bedroom at Willy's house, the one I had stayed in a few days before. I must have been dreaming, I thought. I lay there, eyes closed, until, after a few minutes, I heard the sound of the door latch turning.

"Friedrich?" Willy crossed the room and approached the bed. "How are you, Friedrich?"

"I don't know." I felt confused. "What am I doing here?"

"You've had quite an experience. We can talk about it when you feel a bit better."

I sat up, resting my head against the headboard. "When are we going to Worms?"

"We've been to Worms already. Don't you remember?" Willy looked slightly astonished.

"My God," I said, surprised. "Of course, I'd forgotten." In an instant I remembered us walking about in the twilight, through the Dom Platz. I remembered talking with Valerie on the lobby phone.

"Then what am I doing here?" Now I felt very confused. "The last thing I recall is going out to get something to eat, a restaurant near . . . Neumarkt." My memory grew rapidly clearer. "I paid the check and headed for the door . . . and then . . ." I stopped, even though my mind raced on . . . Matthew Holbein . . . the crowds and the soldiers . . . the crypt . . . Anna Katherine. There was no way to begin . . . and Willy was talking.

"You apparently collapsed on the way back to the hotel, Friedrich. When you didn't return in a reasonable time, I went looking for you. When I found you in the

Dom Platz you were unconscious. It was about two thirty A.M. I must say, when I roused you, you were in quite an agitated state, rambling on. I took you to the emergency room at the hospital. The doctor checked you over. You were still agitated, and he wanted to keep you for observation, but I finally persuaded him to let me bring you back here and have my own physician examine you. Neither doctor found anything wrong with you physically. So I was advised to let you rest. Which is what I have done."

"How long have I been out of it?"

"It was yesterday morning that I found you."

"And today is . . .?"

"Friday."

"My God. You mean to tell me I've been lying here, like this, for twenty-four hours?" After the first shock, I was furious.

"The point is, Friedrich, you're safe."

"Of course I'm safe." Then, demandingly: "Let me have my clothes."

Willy opened the armoire, pointed to my things hanging there, and said, "I'll see you downstairs. We can have some breakfast."

The ham and eggs were exquisite. I ate ravenously, like someone who had not eaten in weeks.

"Sorry I was abrupt with you upstairs, Willy," I said, "but I'm sure you can understand how disconcerting this whole thing is."

"Of course I understand," he replied. Then, thoughtfully, he asked, "Do you want to call it off?"

"Call what off?"

"This search into Fridericus."

"Call it off?" He had touched a nerve with his question. "Why would I want to call it off?"

"Perhaps it is too disturbing for you in your present state of mind." Now he sounded like Mort Stein.

"For Christ's sake, you and Adam Rheinhart are the ones who suggested it in the first place. You know that if it hadn't been for that crazy episode in New York, I wouldn't even be here. What are you suggesting? That I write it all off to a nervous breakdown and go home?"

"Maybe that's all it has been after all," Willy said. "Nerves." He sounded neither convinced nor convincing.

"You don't think that for a minute, Gutheim." I was furious again. "Why are you talking this way?"

He stood up, walked over to the electric percolator, and poured himself another cup of coffee.

"Because we don't really know enough. Because the risk is very high."

"You and Rheinhart have tossed the words 'risk' and 'dangerous' around pretty loosely, it seems to me, and without any explanation. What risk are you talking about?"

Willy had sat down again. He pushed his chair away from the table. "If what you have been going through has anything to do with reincarnation," he began, "and note that I say '*if*,' then we are tampering with forces that we barely understand."

"It's a hell of a time to acknowledge that," I said, sarcastically.

"Hear me out, Friedrich. There are risks either way. Obviously it has been our intention to take you over the same ground, into the very places where the original Fridericus lived, in the hope of stimulating some kind of recognition within you of another self. This has been for the primary purpose of seeing whether, through such contact, you yourself could gain greater control over the influence of the past and thus free yourself from its hold."

"Now you sound like a psychiatrist," I said.

"We have never done this before."

"Now you tell me!"

Willy weighed his words carefully. "We have never before found a subject in the early stages of disintegration."

I could say nothing. His word "disintegration" struck me with the force and futility a patient must feel when told he has a malignancy that is probably inoperable.

"I don't know what you're talking about, Willy."

"We feel certain that reincarnation itself is a reality. The spirit does not die with the body, but goes on and is sooner or later born again on earth. Many cultures have built religions around this concept; its adherents number into the millions in India alone. Reinhart, Henderson, myself, others have been trying to look at it as a natural phenomenon, trying to discover laws that govern it, attempting to define a scientific basis for it that can be understood more and more as our knowledge of physics and the natural sciences expands."

"And?"

"I'm primarily a theoretician, Friedrich. Rheinhart is an experimentalist. Currently he's focusing on hypnosis. Also, his group is trying to identify and classify the many patterns that may be lumped together under the catchall term 'reincarnation.' Most of my work has been spent trying to integrate the concept of reincarnation with theories and facts derived from other disciplines—neuropsychology, information theory, physics, for instance."

"In other words, you think you have a theory to explain what I've been going through?"

167

"I have developed what I call the concept of fusion. Consider. You and I are full human beings. If we lived before, we must have had a completeness then as well. Death destroys the integrity of mind and body, liberating the spirit, whatever that may be, and that spirit may then be reintegrated, whenever and for whatever reason, within a new physical form. If so, it must find that form, choosing somehow the time and place of rebirth. And once it does, the next union of spirit and form must have its totality so that, even though the spirit is the same, the new personality has its own autonomy and uniqueness."

"What has this to do with me?" I asked, though I really didn't want to know. If Mort Stein had been right, if I was really in a highly vulnerable emotional state, the more information I had, the less I would be able to keep myself in one piece.

"I am convinced," said Gutheim, "that in a certain number of cases the fusion to the new personality is faulty, incomplete, fragile—use whatever word you want—and that under the right circumstances the process can reverse itself."

"You mean that the former personality will take over the present one or something like that?" I began to think that he was building his case on the kind of psychological evidence that had long since been proved to be hysteria. Multiple personalities. *Three Faces of Eve. Sybil.*

Willy had anticipated me. "I am not referring to the kind of multiple personality that you psychiatrists are familiar with, where one or more other selves can be found to have originated in severe childhood traumas. I'm talking about a real reversion, in time and space, to one's former self. In your case, you would not adopt the experiences and personality of Fridericus in your present life, entirely or even partly. You would literally become Fridericus in his own time."

"And just what would happen to the me here and now?"

Again, it was a question I did not want to ask but felt compelled to.

"Frederic Pleier would vanish."

"You mean disappear in a puff of smoke . . .?" I snapped my fingers, angrily. "Like so?"

"Not quite like so," Willy said, repeating my gesture. "Sometimes, perhaps, it might happen that way. Saying good-bye to one's family in the morning and going to get the train and never arriving at one's destination and simply never being seen again. But most of the time, I believe, only after a period of severe emotional distress, resembling, sometimes, the more catastrophic breakdowns that psychiatrists deal with regularly. Or perhaps, less dramatically, after a period of depression that may go unnoticed or which the individual may try to explain entirely in terms of contemporary personal problems."

"That's madness! And what happens to the body?"

"If the spirit goes, under these circumstances, the physical form disappears as well."

"That's against every rule of matter. It's impossible."

"If you hold to the preatomic-age viewpoint of matter, perhaps. But we're not even sure what matter is. Time itself—as we divide and calibrate it—may prove to be an artifical construct. Perhaps all time is one."

"Are you telling me that my patients are really suffering from a kind of incomplete reincarnation fusion, that that is the basis of their illness? I've never heard such an absurdity."

"Of course not. I am saying," he went on emphatically, "that in some instances what you call illness and the disintegration of a reincarnation fusion may be practically indistinguishable."

"I'm glad you're willing to set some limits on this theory of yours," I said. Then, suddenly, for the first time since I had awakened, I felt a terrible wave of fear engulf me at the thought of Matthew's disappearance.

"I don't expect you to believe what I am proposing," Willy was saying, "but I am asking you not to ignore the possibility. And for your own sake realize that, if this is what you have been struggling with, we must use unusual methods to try to halt the process . . . if we can."

The wave of fear was reaching panic proportions as I remembered all the events leading up to the horror of my birthday night in New York. I tried to reassure myself that that awful experience was the reason I had called Rheinhart in the first place. That was why I had been willing to come here to Germany and go with Willy to Worms.

Worms.

What did Willy mean, "unusual methods"? Could he have already used those methods in Worms? What if I had really been in a delirium caused by some experimental drug he had given me? For the first time I could not be sure I trusted him. I decided I had better not tell him what I remembered of the night before last.

We walked out onto Willy's terrace overlooking the old town below. "Willy," I said, "tell me what happened in Worms."

"I already told you."

"What else happened? What haven't you told me?"

"Nothing."

"You're lying."

"I found you near the wall of the Jewish cemetery, just as I told you."

"You said you found me in the Dom Platz."

"I made a mistake. You were near the cemetery."

"You're too precise to make a mistake like that, Gutheim, unless you're trying to conceal something. And you said I was 'rambling on' that night. What was I saying?" What had I already told him? "I want to know exactly everything that took place."

"I have told you everything I can," he said firmly.

"Then why are you backing away from your intention to look into this further? I think you're the one who wants to call it off."

He was annoyed. "I am not backing away. I only think that you have reached another decision point. You must share in the choice of whether or not to pursue the experiments further, now that you more fully understand the danger involved."

"Understand?" I shouted. "Understand? I don't understand any of this, Gutheim. How can you expect me to understand? What are you trying to do? Drive me crazy?" I was trembling. It must be some kind of conspiracy, I thought. Gutheim and Rheinhart and who else? Why? What motive could there be? Why would they want to drive me insane or convince me I had regressed to take on the identity of someone who lived three hundred and fifty years ago?

"Please, Friedrich. Calm down."

"Calm down?" I began to pace back and forth on the terrace. "You tell me I may be disintegrating. You reassure me by informing me you've never seen anyone in what you call an early phase of losing his reincarnation fix and that you're really not sure what to do about it

171

except expose me to things and places from the past and hope I'll give you some clue to the cure. And then you say that if I want to, I can call the whole thing off, head for the airport, fly home, and pick up my life where I left off, only there's a good chance that when the plane lands in New York I won't be on it. I'll have vanished! One of us has to be mad, Gutheim, or maybe both of us. Or maybe there's something else going on that I don't know about. What the hell choice are you giving me?"

There was a steep drop from the terrace to a road, some few hundred feet below. For a split second I thought, Go ahead, jump. That will end this nightmare. Or maybe it's all a nightmare—standing here, and Willy, and being in Germany at all. Maybe I'll wake up and Valerie will be lying there next to me and I'll take her hand and everything will be all right again.

"You must choose, Friedrich."

I pulled myself together. "All right, Willy. If I do agree to spend a few more days with you, searching this thing out, what do you have in mind?"

He smiled his big smile, looking relieved. "Come into the library," he said. He sounded curiously eager. What was he going to spring on me?

Taking several sheets of paper from a large manila envelope, he waved to me to sit down behind his desk, stood beside me, and gave me the documents to read.

"These are addressed to A. Emmanuel Stupanus, Professor of Medicine at the University of Basel at the time of Fridericus. They are copies, of course. The originals are in the library at Basel. But look . . ."

The topmost sheet was the first page of a letter. Willy's finger moved to the name Stupanus. He then turned several pages over and pointed to the end—to the final signature: Fridericus Pleiert.

"Where did you get these?"

"Your friend Professor Heimwich. I approached him before you even arrived here to see if I could obtain information about Fridericus, and when I learned the name of Fridericus's professor, I asked if he could conveniently check records under the same Stupanus and, should he discover anything relevant to Fridericus, send it on to me."

"And he agreed?" It was hard for me to envision the stolid Heimwich cooperating with a parapsychologist.

"I told him I was tracing your genealogy." Willy grinned.

Strangely, the fear and desperation I had felt on the terrace were dissolving somewhat. Willy's theories, though still troubling to me, seemed increasingly preposterous. His reference to Heimwich had helped, somehow, to restore my sense of reality, and sitting there, holding in my hands IBM copies of the old documents, helped to reestablish a degree of perspective. I could see some secretary in Basel dispassionately running them through the copying machine, totally indifferent to their contents.

Willy had said I had to choose whether to go on with the search or not. I had to make the choice and I had agreed to do so, for a few more days at any rate. He had practically admitted that he had not been entirely truthful with me regarding our trip to Worms, but then, I was not being truthful with him either. I'd give it a few more days. After that, if nothing turned up, I'd go back home and call Mort Stein for an appointment and tell him what had happened, apologize—although one really does not have to apologize to one's analyst—for my foolishness, and begin active therapy again. For the moment, however, the letters aroused my curiosity.

"These are in Latin," I observed. "Mine's pretty rusty. Do you know what's in them?"

"We will shortly," Willy looked at his watch. "I've had one of my assistants translate them into English, and now that you seem interested, I'll call her and ask her to bring the translations over. She's quite pretty," he added. "I'll ask her to stay to dinner."

Willy Gutheim's father had died when he was only eight, I thought to myself, and his mother had devoted the rest of her life to a neurotic need for constant reassurances that her husband was still with her, at least in spirit. Willy's theory on reincarnation fusion could well be the result of a small child's anguish over suddenly losing a father he adored.

A question suddenly occurred to me. "While we're waiting," I said, "tell me one thing. Is there an American army base in Worms?"

"I really don't know," Willy replied.

~ 17 ~

WILLY'S ASSISTANT, HELENA, ARRIVED WITHIN AN HOUR WITH the translated letters. There were three in all, one dated in 1632, the second in 1636 and the final one, 1640. Each was addressed "My dear Stupanus" and signed "Fridericus Pleiert." But as we compared the original documents with the typed translations, it was at once apparent that the writer's handwriting had changed dramatically from a bold and well-defined form in the first two letters to little more than a scrawl in the third.

The first letter was dated April 3, 1632. Willy read the tranlation aloud.

> My dear Stupanus:
> My journey back to Worms was without the hardships and fear of my way to you but a year ago. Nevertheless, that which I saw filled me with horror and sadness. Everywhere from Mulhouse north to Strasbourg and on to Worms the countryside has been devastated. Where there were villages, there are villages no more. In Strasbourg I learned that in the cold of the winter past, tens of thousands of poor lay in

the streets, sick and dying, until the magistrates forced them at gunpoint to leave and starve in the wilderness. Soldiers move about without discipline or order, taking as they will what they will. God's fortune that I passed among them untouched, like a beggar.

Here there is little left. What was once a great city of thousands is barely alive. What the fighting has not ruined, the lack of food has, and what desperate starvation has not taken, the plague has.

To my great sadness, Anna Katherine and my daughters have gone (died) of plague, my younger daughter, Katherine, only a few days after my return. So, too, the good Jacob. What I hoped would be safety for them has proved their ending. I have only Matthius left, and my purpose, and in that I feel often impotent. What remedies would even Paracelsus offer for populace (social) madness?

I sat with Katherine for hours, easing her pain and fear as I could, hoping at moments I too might succumb to pestilence and join her. I bathed her fever and soothed her swollen body until the last moment of life was gone and I felt the full sadness of it all for the first time, nor would it go away. I tell you this, for I have no one but you to share my grief.

There are rumors of peace. If true, a blessing. It is heard that John George stands for it, clearly, though his strength may not be sufficient. The Emperor gains strength. It matters to me not who conquers, only that it end. In Basel, you may know more.

The peace of Basel seems so far away. I think of Petergasse and the quiet house and the (coherence?) and you pleading with me to stay and I forfeiting all to come to Anna and children.

When I was your student I sought to help
those maddened with affliction of mind. Now.I
do not know, truly, verily, who they are and who
are not.
All that is left is to build again, and, perhaps,
to learn to pray to what God there is.
                                    With deep respect,
                                    Fridericus Pleiert

The three of us sat there, silently.

"Well?" Willy asked. "What do you think?"

"Let's see," I said. "We already know Fridericus went to Worms in 1623. He must have made a trip from Worms to Basel early in 1631—'but a year ago,' it says here, just under the April 1632 date—during the wars. He left his wife and family behind. That wife was Anna Katherine, whom he'd married in 1621. Apparently his wife and older daughter died before his return, then his daughter Katherine and 'the good Jacob', shortly after."

"And later," Willy said, "according to the records you showed me from Worms, his second wife was Christina, recorded as godmother in 1633." Willy looked at me strangely. "What are you thinking, Friedrich?"

"Nothing. Nothing at all." In fact, the name Jacob had struck a chord in me. It sounded familiar. I felt a wave of sadness. "Just that it sounds like a hell of a time to be alive."

The image of the doctor, still a young man—he would have been about thirty-seven at the time—holding his dying child in his arms, rashly disregarding infection, hoping to die himself, was a devastating one, and I could not help but be moved.

Willy began to read the second letter, dated February 12, 1638.

My dear Stupanus:
It goes on, as if forever. There is no peace. Because I am a physician I am allowed to survive, though for what purpose I know not. Christina has proved a good wife. My son, Matthius, is fifteen and, though thin, strong. The French are here, and better ordered than before. They give us food—I being a physician—though often little more than roots. But for the rest, they must seek it as they can.

The bodies of criminals have been torn from the gallows and devoured and recent graves molested. (illegible) go in terror of being attacked and killed for eating. Children that lack protection of family vanish, their fate a horror.

I wish not to belabor you with what transpires but I know not who else to tell. God has cursed us. Never has the winter been so cold, nor crops so few or ravaged by troops. The pestilence awaits us again in the spring.

I am sorely tempted to die. To escape is not possible, for only by my (vocation?) life permitted. Nor have I energy. Nor will I take the risk, for Christina and Matthius could not (illegible) the journey south.

There is some joy, though small. I heal some who can be healed. At Christmas all, no matter the direction of their faith, together came to worship. In the evening, I (sit?) with my son and tell him of the world as it was and, though hope is slight, will be again.

The will to survive is indeed an incredible (instinct?).

That this river is the one and same that passes beneath the Rheinbrucke by your window is difficult to believe.

Remember me, my friend and teacher, and
in your prayers.

> With deep respect,
> Fridericus Pleiert

When he had finished reading, Willy looked at me.
"What is it, Friedrich?"

"Nothing."

"You look stricken."

"Something I'm trying to remember." Willy's voice
reading "this river is the one and same . . . " had taken
me back to the vision of another river passing by a window—to Mort Stein's office way back last fall, when I told
him my dream of the house overlooking the river. But I
did not want to make the connection for Willy at that moment. It was too real, and I still could not bring myself
to trust him. "It'll come to me, I guess. Is there one more
letter?"

"I'll read it," he said. "It's quite brief, dated June
4, 1640."

> Stupanus:
>   We still live, I and Matthius, though not
> Christina. I have learned that the Englishman
> Harvey has used the incubating eggs of chickens
> to show that blood does circulate and the heart
> acts as pump.
>   There may yet be a future.
>
> Fridericus

I sat there silently, thinking of Fridericus, still more
moved than I could say. That he bore my name, that I
was here in quest of information that might shed light
on the issue of what strange way he and I might be con-
nected made the impact of his words even greater. What

would he have been had he lived under other circumstances? Born during the death throes of feudalism, too
soon for rationalism and the Enlightenment, he had brutal
mercenaries and murdered peasants as his daily experience
and Harvey as nothing more than a fragile hope of things
to come. I thought of his treatise on melancholy, his struggling to comprehend humanely and scientifically the mentally disturbed of his era. What a topic to choose—one
that would forecast the shadows of the rest of his life. I
thought of a line I had read in his thesis, something about
the true art of healing being prevention. I thought of the
letters again, and could reach out and touch his despair.

"Well?" Willy asked again.

"I can see why he felt entitled to a second chance,"
I replied.

~ 18 ~

HELENA STAYED FOR DINNER. THE PLAYFULNESS OF THEIR conversation—although often in German and beyond my comprehension—nevertheless betrayed, by its warmth and humor, a considerable degree of intimacy, and it was obvious that Helena was more than just another technician. And, as Willy had said, she was lovely—tall, lithe, with blond hair—and to me a sort of a German variation of Valerie.

I phoned home. It was three thirty in the afternoon, Friday, May 5, in New York. I told Valerie I'd be home Monday, in the late afternoon. She sounded distant.

Willy poured himself some brandy and lit a cigar. I had a crème de menthe. Helena had gone home.

"There's still nothing conclusive," I said.

"Nothing is ever conclusive," Willy retorted.

"I've been giving your ideas some thought," I said. "If reincarnation is a reality and if, in some cases, the process is confused and becomes reversible . . . obviously, it isn't in most . . . what determines whether the fusion holds or not? If I am in danger, as you think I may be, of some kind of reversion, why me? Have you figured that out yet?"

181

"No. I haven't yet had enough cases to study closely to do more than speculate broadly on what might account for a reversal. But I have some hunches. It must have to do with some quality in the life—or death—of the person you are or the person you were. Something could be pulling you back, maybe—though considering the terrible conditions of Fridericus's life, it's hard to imagine what. Some unfinished business, perhaps? Or perhaps your being a psychiatrist, delving into yourself while probing into the minds of others, thereby loosening—as one might put it—the boundaries of your soul."

"Everyone who is analyzed and every psychiatrist is involved in that kind of process. And they certainly don't fall apart."

"I've read that psychiatrists have the highest rate of depression and suicide of any occupational group."

"But they don't"—I used the word with a mixture of apprehension and contempt—"dematerialize."

"Friedrich," Willy said strongly. "Not everyone on this earth has been reincarnated, necessarily. For one thing, it would seem that there are some basic mathematical problems involved—there are simply too many people now living for all of them to have been reincarnated. And there probably are other options than reincarnation for life after death. The whole point of our work is to avoid rigid formulas and keep an open mind."

"You don't know how it happens, but you're still sure it does."

"Absolutely."

"Your faith amazes me, Willy. Sometimes you almost have me believing you."

"Almost?"

"Enough to scare me at times. Enough to make me

go along with you and see this thing out, for a few more days at least. As I said. What's next on your agenda?"

"A peaceful weekend. I've taken the liberty of making reservations for us in Baden-Baden, at Brenner's Park Hotel." He poured himself another brandy. "The food is marvelous," he continued, "and the waters are supposed to be healing. And in the evening we can go gambling at the casino."

"Willy," I said firmly. "I don't have time to waste on a 'peaceful' weekend. I intend to go back to New York Monday afternoon at the latest. My wife is expecting me."

"Don't worry—that will be fine. We can drive to Basel Sunday from Baden-Baden in a couple of hours. Even Monday morning is time enough. You can catch a flight to Zurich or drive, and fly home from there. As for our research, I will have one more thing to show you."

"What is that?"

"I'd rather keep it as a surprise." Still feeling the impact of Fridericus's letters, I was somewhat nervous over Willy's surprises, but I felt no desire to press the question.

"Baden-Baden is largely nineteenth and twentieth century," he called to me as I went upstairs to the bedroom. "There will be no associations for Fridericus. We can be sure of relative peace."

Normally I too had a keen sense of humor, but it had fled me almost entirely during the last few days. I supposed Willy could keep his, even in the face of what he thought to be a grave crisis. For one thing, he was the professional. And for another, he wasn't the one faced with the prospect of vanishing.

My mind teemed with pictures . . . my eating dinner so innocently in Worms, and then suddenly the church bells, the mad crowd, the burning of the old woman . . .

the city on fire . . . the priest pulling me into a tunnel . . . waking up crouched against a wall, afraid of being killed . . . what was it Willy had let slip? He had found me in the Jewish cemetery.

Why did "the good Jacob," in Fridericus's letter, affect me so deeply? It had sounded so familiar.

And Matthius—in all three letters—my God, I thought. Matthew Holbein, sitting in the hospital room, telling me that *I* knew what was happening to him, tearing at his bandages and biting his arm as if to reassure himself that he was still there, and finally running away and never being found. If he had drowned in the river, his body would surely have shown up someplace. If he hadn't, where the hell was he?

Willy was ninety-five percent home. With the remaining five percent of my rational mind I clung desperately to thoughts of Valerie and the children.

The weekend at Baden-Baden was, surprisingly, a delight, as Willy had promised. Brenner's Park Hotel was exquisitely maintained and had all the charm that made it known as one of the world's greatest hotels. At the casino, I won forty marks at roulette, while Willy discovered a tall, red-haired, unattached Frenchwoman at the blackjack tables. In the BMW we made it to Basel in three hours flat. As we passed signs pointing west to Strasbourg and Colmar and Mulhouse, I thought of its taking Fridericus weeks, perhaps months, surrounded by horror and wreckage, to traverse the same distance.

The girl at the desk of the Three Kings was the same one who had been there the previous September. Was it only seven months since Heimwich had given me that damned thesis, since we had all been sitting over there on the terrace, overlooking the Rhine? I had found Basel unusually pleasant and peaceful then and I did again now. What was it Fridericus had said in his letter to Stupanus? Oh, yes, that the "peace of Basel seems so far away. I think of Petersgasse and the quiet house . . ."

"It's only a five-minute walk from the hotel, " Willy announced the next morning, shoving me through the front doors of the Three Kings onto the street. He seemed ebullient.

My eye caught the sign on the bridge crossing the river. It was the Rheinbrucke.

"This way," he gestured, climbing up a long narrow street that ran parallel to the Rhine, separated from the river only by a set of ancient buildings. Halfway up he stopped in front of a building which must have been a home at one time. On the exterior of the wall, over the front door, in recently painted blue and red lettering, was the word *Flachlander* and the date 1619. To the right of the door was a brass plaque that read, ANDREAS MUSEUM. He led me inside.

He spoke for a minute with the attendant, pulled two Swiss francs from his pocket, handed them to him, and then, pointing to a marble staircase, led me upstairs. We entered a room that was obviously devoted to relics of the late medieval and early Renaissance periods. There was a model of the city of Basel in the year 1689. Crossbows and old muskets were neatly placed and labeled behind glass cabinets. At various parts of the room, flags and emblems were poised erect, some tattered, many still in unbelievably fresh condition.

He had already reached the far end of the large room and waved to me to come. "Look," he said triumphantly.

185

The painting was labeled "The Physicians, circa 1600–1650." A group of men dressed in black, with thick white ruffled collars and white lace at their wrists, stood stiffly around a bare table. Willy pointed to one of the figures and told me to look at it closely. He was wearing a flat black hat, like a beret. His eyes, looking straight out at the viewer, were sad, and his expression was one of thoughtfulness.

"Remove the beard, add a couple of pounds, and what do we have here?" Willy asked rhetorically.

Do you know, do you have any idea what it is like to look at a painting three hundred and some odd years old and see an almost exact likeness of yourself? I could hear the roulette wheel at the casino tumbling from hole to hole, until it stopped and the croupier shouted, "Twenty-five red," but this croupier was chanting in my head, over and over again, louder and louder, "Willy wins, Willy wins, Willy wins."

I could think of nothing to say.

~ 19 ~

FOR MOST OF THE WAY BACK TO NEW YORK, I WAS PREOC-
cupied with Willy's speculations on the reversibility of reincarnation. I tried to distract myself by reading a Travis
McGee thriller and carrying on a conversation with a
banker in the seat next to me about gold markets and
inflation hedges. I dozed a bit, but as soon as I would
close my eyes, the painting would appear before me, and
Fridericus would stare out at me as if he were about to
speak.

Even before we had left the museum, Willy had begun to give me specific instructions. He was going to have
a photo of the painting taken and send it on to Rheinhart.
I was to contact Rheinhart as soon as I reached New York
and arrange to meet with him as soon as possible. Willy
would inform him, in detail, of what we had unearthed.

"Be sure to call Rheinhart as soon as you are home,
Friedrich," Willy had repeated at the airport as I was about
to board the plane. "And please, do understand the urgency of your situation."

For a moment, standing there clasping his big hand,
I had no reservations whatsoever about anything he was

saying. Now, though, I told myself that words such as "urgency" were overstated. And at last, as the plane got closer and closer to New York, my attention turned more and more to what I was going to tell Valerie.

I decided to level with her.

She was waiting for me at the international arrivals building at Kennedy. The sight of her lifted my spirits, as it always did.

"You look tired, darling," she said, reaching to take my briefcase. "Are you all right?"

"Long flight. A good night's sleep will help." I added. "But *you* look really great."

Valerie drove our white Volvo, heading up the Van Wyck Expressway to pick up the Long Island Expressway and head into Manhattan through the Midtown Tunnel. She chatted on, about what she had been doing, a film she had seen, lunch with Margaret, a birthday party for one of Jenny's classmates . . . and then she came to the question.

"How were the meetings?"

"Okay." I saw a sign for Forest Hills. Either I start making up a story, I thought, or I tell her, now. "Valerie," I began. I'd kept my eyes on her—I liked watching her drive.

"All right, Frederic," she said, looking straight ahead, "what is it you want to get off your chest?" She always used my full name for special effect.

"There were no meetings, at least not the kind I said I was going for. I lied to you. I'm sorry."

"What were you doing?"

"Rheinhart suggested it. Adam Rheinhart. You recall, he was at Margaret's."

"And?"

"Before you jump to conclusions, let me tell you the whole story."

"Before I jump to conclusions! My God, Fred. I've been worried for months about you. Do you really think you fooled me? I suspected you'd involved yourself with Rheinhart, and that your trip to Europe had something to do with this Fridericus business."

"You knew?"

"Of course I knew. Do you really think two people could be as close as we've been and that I wouldn't sense what's been going on?"

"Valerie." I put my hand on her arm. "Let me tell you what has happened. Please."

"Not now, Fred." There were tears in her eyes. "Let's get home in one piece first. Then I'll have a drink and we can sit down and you can tell me everything."

She paid the toll and we pulled into the tunnel. It was 9 P.M. and dark when we arrived at the apartment.

Valerie was true to her word. She fixed herself a Bloody Mary and poured a light Scotch for me, while I took my suitcase upstairs. When I came down again, she was sitting in the living room, waiting.

She looked neither frightened nor angry. She just looked sad. "All right, darling. Tell me . . . what happened?"

I took a deep breath. "From the beginning?"

"Start anywhere," she said. "It doesn't matter."

I tried to organize my thoughts.

"There's this German, Willy Gutheim. He's a friend of Rheinhart's, an expert in reincarnation. After that business of my birthday . . . you remember?"

"How could I forget?"

"Well, after that, I called Rheinhart and he and I

met and he thought I had to look into the reincarnation possibility actively. He urged me to meet Gutheim and travel with him to the places Fridericus had been, to see if that would stimulate anything."

Valerie listened patiently but with obvious astonishment at realizing how far things had gone. I felt myself becoming agitated.

"We found some old letters . . . that Fridericus wrote to his professor in Basel." I felt confused, disjointed. "And then there was the painting. It was incredible, Val, it looked just like me."

"Take it easy, Fred. Just tell me, a bit at a time."

I decided to do it chronologically, relating our journey from my arrival at Zurich to Worms and finally the museum in Basel.

"What happened in Worms?"

"I don't recall. It's a blank." I lied. I couldn't find the words to tell her. "Willy says I was out for about twenty-four hours." I couldn't share my suspicions about Willy with her either.

"Does Mort Stein know you intended to go?"

I felt a flash of anger. "No," I answered, defensively.

Until then, she had been hiding her fear. Suddenly she stood up, walked toward the window, turned quickly around, and shouted, "He's your doctor, Fred. Don't you realize there is something wrong with you?"

"There's nothing wrong, Valerie!"

"Nothing wrong? You tell me that you have amnesia for twenty-four hours or more, that you've mixed yourself up with people who think you may be involved in some kind of crazy reincarnation collapse and in danger of vanishing, and you tell me there is nothing wrong! This is your second episode of amnesia, Fred. I'm terrified."

"First."

She was seated again. "Second. The night of your birthday, the experience you say prompted you to call Rheinhart in the first place. Have you forgotten?"

"No. I recall everything about that night."

"You mean you remember?"

"I didn't want to frighten you."

"Well, you've succeeded in scaring me half to death." She appeared stunned.

"I'm not a fool, Val. I didn't call Rheinhart on a whim. Mort Stein told me to drop it. I did, for months. But when I had that . . . nightmare . . . I felt I had to explore the possibility that I might be involved in some parapsychological phenomenon. With people like Rheinhart believing that things like that occur, I couldn't just dismiss them with a stock answer."

She sat there, silently, looking helpless and defeated. "I don't know what to think, Fred, except that I love you and I don't want anything to happen to you . . . to us."

"I'll tell you what I'll do. I'll call Stein in the morning, see him tomorrow if he can take me, and go over the whole thing with him."

"And Rheinhart?"

"I don't know. I promised to call him. I don't think I should close that option, not yet, at any rate. There are too many unexplained issues."

"Every one of which is inconclusive," Valerie interrupted.

"How do you explain the portrait?"

"Fred. For heaven's sake. If I were to wander through museums and galleries I'm sure I'd find one with a strong likeness to me too. I'm sure most of us could, if we stretch our imaginations a little bit."

"If that were all . . ."

"Just call Stein in the morning. Please. Keep your promise. And please, Fred don't . . . exclude me, ever again." She looked at me, waiting.

I had to say I wouldn't.

I locked the front door while Valerie cleaned up a few things in the kitchen. We went upstairs to bed.

In the dim glow of the lights from the bridge outside the window, I could see Valerie lying on the bed in her blue cotton pajamas, staring at the ceiling. I walked across the room and sat down beside her, taking her hand, which tightened around my own. But when I leaned over to kiss her, she drew away.

"I'm sorry, darling," I said. "I really am. I need you, Valerie. I need to be close to you."

Her response was instantaneous. She reached up and pulled me toward her. "You've been so terribly far away," she whispered, as I felt the warmth and excitement welling through her body.

I was safe again in her arms. My own passion grew stronger with hers, with the sense of oneness. . . .

For several minutes afterward, we lay there in silence, holding each other.

"I've missed you so much," she murmured in my ear. "I love you, Friedrich."

Friedrich! I started. That's not Valerie's voice! I looked at her face. She was smiling. My God, that's not Valerie's face!

I sat bolt upright, reached for the light switch, and turned it on.

"What are you doing, Fred? What is it?"

It was Valerie all right, stunned, pulling the sheet up to cover herself.

"Sorry, Val. But for an instant . . . I don't know. Forgive me. I was confused."

She leaned forward and kissed me on the cheek. "Let's go to sleep," she said. "I'm exhausted. You must be too."

"In a few minutes. I'm going to go down and get a glass of milk."

I took my milk and the pile of mail from the hall table and went into the living room to glance through it. I had to clear my head. For a moment, upstairs, I had thought that Valerie was someone else. I had to shake it off. Tomorrow I'd call Stein, as I promised. And Rheinhart.

There was an invitation for us to go to the opening of a new play, some kind of benefit. The Con Edison and Bell Telephone bills. A postcard from Japan from a friend of Val's and a brochure from our travel agent describing a new Caribbean resort and urging us to make our reservations early. I don't know what I'll be doing this month, much less next winter, I thought. I heard Valerie calling.

"Coming up to bed?"

"Soon," I called back.

"Fred?"

"Yes, darling?"

She had come downstairs and was standing in the hall, looking directly at me, into the living room. "Fred? Where are you?"

"Right here."

She came into the room, walked within ten feet of me and right past into the library. Then, swiftly, she came back again and on into the dining room and the kitchen. I could hear a sense of urgency in her voice as she called my name.

I stood up and walked to the hall. "Here, Val."

She came out of the dining room and went up the

stairs. I followed her. When I walked into the bedroom she was reaching for the phone.

"Where have you been?" she said, frantically. "Are you trying to scare me out of my wits?"

"I was downstairs, in the living room, going through the mail."

"Please, Fred. I can't take much more of this. If you don't stop *I'm* going to have a nervous breakdown."

I broke my promise and lied again. "I went out to drop some papers in the incinerator, darling. I'm sorry to give you a scare."

"I'm just wrought up, Fred. I thought you had gone off again . . . when you make the appointment with Mort, ask him if he can see me with you, would you?"

"Of course."

She was asleep in fifteen minutes. It was eleven thirty. I'd been able to calm Valerie down, but I had not been able to do the same for myself. It was the therapist's reaction—soothe the patient; quiet her fears. But my own, that was a different matter.

"Please do understand the urgency of your situation," Willy had cautioned. "Be sure to call Rheinhart as soon as you are home."

I returned downstairs, quietly. It was eight thirty in California. I dialed Rheinhart's number. No answer. I sat there next to the phone, dialing it again and again, every ten minutes for nearly an hour.

Thinking. Valerie had stood right there, in the living room, again in the hall, looking past me, seeing nothing.

We have never seen someone in the early stages of disintegration, Willy had said. He was convinced that the reincarnation process was reversible, if the fusion was faulty, but he did not know what might account for it.

He had taken me everywhere in search of a clue and I had not provided him with one. Crazy. The whole thing is crazy. I'm losing my mind.

I let it ring twenty times. No answer.

If the fusion is inadequate, Willy postulated, I might vanish. People disappear every day and are never seen or heard from again. Valerie had looked at me and had not seen me. That terrible night in Worms—had I actually vanished from the twentieth century during part of the time that Willy was looking for me? What was he holding back? My head began to pound. I dialed again. An operator came on to tell me the call could not be completed as it had been dialed and to dial again. I banged the receiver down, then I picked it up and rang a familiar local number.

A sleepy voice answered.

"Frank Holbein?"

"Yes. Who is this?"

"Fred. Fred Pleier."

"What do you want at this hour?"

"I have to see you."

"Are you out of your mind, Fred? Call me in the morning."

"Frank. I have to see you. I have to talk to you."

"Please, Fred. Leave us alone. Call me tomorrow."

He hung up.

If Matthew Holbein's disappearance had anything to do with Gutheim's speculations, maybe, if I knew more about what had been going on in his life before he became ill, I could find something to shed light on what I too might be going through.

There's no time left, I thought. Rheinhart's not available and I have to find out now. I went quickly upstairs, dressed in an old pair of slacks and a sports shirt, grabbed my raincoat, and went down the elevator out onto the street. At First Avenue I caught a taxi and directed the driver to take me to the Holbein address on Fifth Avenue. I nodded to the doorman, went on up, and rang the apartment buzzer. Frank Holbein answered the door in his bathrobe.

"I told you to call me tomorrow." He was furious.

"You've got to let me in, Frank. I have to talk with you."

"Go home, Fred. For God's sake, go home."

"Frank. I have to know more about Matthew."

"Stop it. You'll wake up Cynthia." He tried to push the door closed. I held it open.

"I'm running out of time, Frank. I have to talk to you."

Reluctantly he released his grip on the door and let me in. "Come into the kitchen, Fred. And be quiet. I don't want to disturb Cynthia."

I sat down at the long plank table in the middle of the large kitchen. Frank sat across from me.

"What is it?" he asked.

"I don't know how to tell you. My life may be in danger. I have to know more about what happened to Matthew. I have to find some kind of connection between what he went through and what I'm going through . . . to save myself." I sounded incoherent, even to myself.

"Don't make me go over it all again, Fred. It's too painful."

"You have to, don't you understand? There may be something in Matt's life that we haven't dug up yet to explain his disappearance."

Frank stared at me. "Are you all right?"

"How would you feel if you thought you might just vanish like Matthew did?"

"I don't know what to say to you, Fred. Don't you think I'd better call Valerie?"

"No!" I knew my voice was too loud, but could hardly control myself.

Frank sounded stern. "If we weren't old friends, Fred, I'd throw you out of here right now. Or call the police. You have to pull yourself together." He took me by the arm. "Let's call Val."

"No!" I shouted. "Frank. Listen . . . when I took the history . . . remember . . . you said something about a game he played, over and over, when he was four or five. He thought he was someone else. There's a man named Henderson who claims small children can be in touch with other existences. I'm talking about reincarnation, Frank. Something may have gone wrong with Matthew's reincarnation and something's gone wrong with mine!"

At that moment Cynthia appeared in the kitchen doorway. She had obviously been listening to most of the conversation. "Get him out of here, Frank," she said emphatically. "Get him out or I *will* call the police!"

I stood up and walked over to her. "Cynthia. I have to know about Matt. Maybe he didn't run away. Maybe he just disappeared. Maybe he was reincarnated and his fusion didn't hold and he went back, into the past, into some other life."

"Frank. Get him out of here! He's mad!"

I reached out and took hold of her bathrobe collar. "Please, Cynthia. You don't understand."

"Get your hands off me!" She pulled away and ran into the other room.

197

I turned to Frank. "You've got to hear me out, Frank. You may be the only one who can give me some answers. I have to find out what's going wrong!"

"All right, Fred. Sit down! What do you want to know?"

"Was there anything strange or unusual going on in his life just before he became psychotic?"

"We've been over that with you and the other doctors before, Fred. You know as much as I do." Frank looked especially tired. "Don't you think you should go home, Fred?"

I was shaking uncontrollably. "Frank. You have to help me. If I don't find out what's happening, I may cease to exist."

At that moment I heard a noise behind me. Turning quickly, I saw a tall blond-haired policeman standing in the kitchen doorway. He walked in, followed by his partner. The two of them stood calmly, a few feet away from me.

"Mrs. Holbein said there was some trouble here," the blond officer said. "What seems to be the matter?"

I didn't know what to say.

"Dr. Pleier is a friend of ours, officer," Frank offered. "He seems pretty upset."

Cynthia entered the room and stood near the door, no longer looking angry. She had obviously called the doorman and had him hail the patrol car.

"Why don't you just come along with us?" the policeman suggested. It was, of course, an order.

Can this really be happening? I thought. I'd been involved two or three times in scenes like this, going with the police to someone's home to persuade a very disturbed patient to come with us to some hospital. Once, I remembered, there was a man sitting in the middle of his living room with a loaded shotgun, threatening to kill himself, and the police detective and I had taken more than an hour to persuade him to let us have the gun and come along with us.

Could this really be happening to me?

"Gets too much for all of us, sometime or other," said the other policeman. "Nothing to be ashamed of in that."

Some cops, I'd learned over the years, were better than most doctors in a pinch.

"We'll just go over to Lenox Hill emergency and have them check things out and see if you're all right, and then you can go home, Doc," the blond man said, reassuringly.

I felt curiously relieved.

~ 20 ~

SEA VIEW PLANTATION WAS SITUATED ON FIFTY ACRES IN northeast Connecticut, bordering the Sound, not too far from New London. It had been given its euphemistic name in the 1920s to remove some of the negative associations attached to its former one, Northeast Asylum. The main building had been built in the nineteenth century. Its massive red-brick form still stood, proudly on sunny days, ominously in rain, in the center of the grounds, dominating the other buildings in the complex. Clustered around it were several small white-clapboard colonial houses and two very recent contemporary glass-and-fieldstone structures—one a cafeteria, the other for occupational and recreational therapy. Most of the patients lived in the main building, where the doctors also maintained their offices. A few, some of whom were there for the rest of their lives, some of whom were facing imminent release, lived in the smaller houses. There were an outdoor swimming pool and an indoor one as well, a dozen tennis courts, and several sailboats moored at the small dock.

Dave Brixton had arranged for my admission to Sea View. By the time the officers had taken me to the emergency room at Lenox Hill Hospital in their patrol car, its siren and lights pushing traffic out of their way, Frank Holbein had called Valerie. Valerie had called Mort Stein. Both of them were waiting for us when we arrived. Brixton showed up a few minutes later.

A strange mood had come over me. Futility. Resignation. No will to live. In the back of the patrol car I thought, numbly and repetitively, It's all over, it's all over. Lines from one of Antoine de Saint Exupéry's novels flashed through my mind, something about, "We are the defeated and the defeated have no right to speak." One of the policemen turned around from time to time and made a few remarks, trying to be reassuring. I remember he asked if I liked baseball. I did not answer.

"Of course, you can go home, Fred," Mort said, "as soon as the resident finishes his preliminary workup. But I wish you'd consider an alternative, a week or two somewhere, so you can rest up and we can have a chance to pull this whole thing together."

One look at the sadness and pain on Valerie's face and I knew I could not go home. Dave phoned the director of Sea View.

"It's far enough away and off the beaten track," he said. "I'll see that your patients are covered. You'll be out and back at work before anyone knows."

I nodded, saying nothing. I wanted to say "I'm sorry" to Valerie, but I couldn't find the energy. She was going to ride with me in the ambulance to Connecticut, but Mort dissuaded her.

"Let him get a few days' rest. You can go up on the weekend. Besides, you don't want to alarm the kids if you can help it."

Maybe they could keep it a secret to the world at

large, but the fact that I was a psychiatrist and that I was now on the admission ward of Sea View Plantation, on constant observation, followed about everywhere by a friendly male orderly, was instant news to the patients and staff. The head nurse made a point of letting me know that no exceptions to the rules could be made on my account, and I told her I realized that and it didn't matter anyway. The doctor on call did a routine physical examination; when he tapped my knee and could elicit no response, he said softly, casually, but quite intentionally, "Battle fatigue." It was meant to reassure me that I was not losing my mind and that I would be fine. Then he muttered something about having read several of my research papers and how impressed he was by them.

There were no individual rooms on the admission unit. Everyone slept on a cot in a large dormitory. The few belongings you were permitted to keep were stowed in a footlocker under the cot. There were twenty patients in all, all men, all admitted to Sea View during the previous few days. It was possible in this way for the nurse on duty to observe the entire group during the night from her station. Adjacent to the dormitory was a dayroom, equally large, where you could sit, watch television, read if able, and converse if motivated. If, after a few days, the doctors felt it was safe enough, you were transferred to a private of semiprivate room on another floor, where, besides having more freedom, you could also socialize with the women patients and eat in the common dining room.

I felt that whatever vestige of dignity I had been able to hold on to had finally been stripped away. The wrist tag with my name and hospital number stamped on it only increased my sense of anonymity. Sitting in the dayroom, in the afternoon of my first day there, staring aimlessly into space, watching a young man on some medication shuffling back and forth across the room, hands trembling, saliva drooling from his mouth, I felt dead inside.

I felt a hand on my arm. I turned slowly. An elderly man, unshaven, in a blue-and-white-striped hospital bathrobe, leaned toward me and whispered that he had heard that a doctor had been admitted to the ward and added, if psychiatrists couldn't help themselves, how could they help us? I tried to smile.

"Mr. Pleier." The nurse had entered the room and was calling me. She had obviously been instructed not to use the title, "Doctor." "You're wanted in Pavilion Three."

I stood up and walked toward her. As I did, my male-orderly companion moved toward me. "Let's go," he said. "I'll show you the way."

We walked through a long underground passage. The windows were scattered at twenty-foot intervals and very high, barely overlooking the grass level outside; they were barred. The walls were painted a dull gray. After about five minutes, we came to a small ramp that slanted up and forward into an obviously new corridor, painted yellow, with cheerful graphics and posters. We took a self-service elevator to the third floor and walked a few feet to a door marked INTERVIEW ROOM. The orderly opened it, ushered me inside, left the room, and closed the door behind him.

"Dr. Pleier." A tall man with graying hair, wearing a long white clinic coat, held out his hand to shake mine. I took it limply.

"I'm Ted Harrison. We met a couple of years ago at the psychiatric meetings in Toronto. I've always admired your work." He waved his hand for me to sit down. "How do you feel?" he asked.

"All right," I answered automatically.

"I'm sure we'll have you off the observation ward in a couple of days. It's routine, you understand."

"Yes."

He reached for a pen and pad of lined paper and placed it on his lap. "Why are you here?" he asked.

For a moment I said nothing. Then I replied, "I thought I gave this information to the doctor when I was admitted."

"You did," Harrison answered. "But I'm going to be taking care of you while you are here and, as you must know, I must hear it for myself."

It was standard procedure.

I remained silent.

"Are you depressed?" Harrison asked.

Again, I did not reply. It seemed pointless.

"I spoke with your wife and with Dr. Stein. I do have a pretty good picture of what you've been going through over the last months. But it would help me to hear it from you."

"I don't want to talk about it, not now, anyway."

"Just tell me what you were doing at the Holbeins' apartment, then." He obviously had a great deal of information already, and he was—correctly—trying to get me to talk without using questions that were too leading.

"I don't know," I said.

"The Holbein boy had been your patient, isn't that right? And he ran away from the hospital. And you thought that he might have vanished because of some kind of time warp or reincarnation collapse?"

He'd blown his cover now. He was looking for delusions.

"I don't know," I answered.

"I can't help you if you won't help yourself," he said.

I wanted to scream that it didn't matter, that I didn't care anymore. I was too tired. If something supernatural was going on, I couldn't fight it anyway. And if this was nothing more than a nervous breakdown, then just give me some medication or something and let me get over it. Or let me die.

"I want to die," I said. I could see him writing it down.

"Why?"

"I don't know why. I don't even know if I really want to. It's just that there seems to be no other solution."

"Then you *are* depressed." He sounded almost triumphant, as if he had finally found something to get a grip on.

"If you say so."

Harrison ordered the nurses to start me on antidepressants. For the next few days, religiously, three times a day, they gave me the two tiny tablets and a little water and made some brief comment about the medicine's being good for me and told me to be patient because it would take a while for it to work. Meanwhile, I ate practically nothing. When Valerie came on visiting day, Sunday, she was shocked to see that I had lost nearly ten pounds. My clothes hung on me as if they were several sizes too large.

"Darling," she said, "Dr. Harrison told me you're not trying. Please, you have to, for my sake."

"I'm doing the best I can, Valerie. I'm just so tired all the time. And I feel really hopeless, for the first time. As if I'm up against something I can't beat."

"They're giving you antidepressants. They told me they expect you to be a lot better in a couple of weeks."

We spoke about the children. Valerie assured me my practice was being well taken care of. Margaret and Alfred wanted to visit, but had been told to wait a week or two until I was feeling better.

"Have you heard anything from Rheinhart?" I finally asked.

Valerie looked suddenly annoyed.

"Have you, Val?"

"He's tried to call you a few times. He got me once, at home. I said you were away."

"You didn't tell him what happened?"

"Why should I? If it weren't for him and his ideas, sending you on that wild-goose chase to Europe, you might not be here now."

A wave of despondency rushed through me. "Please, Val. Tell him. I want to see him."

"I will not!" she replied. Then, as if to placate me, she added, "Maybe when you are feeling better and this thing is under control. But not until you have enough strength to know fact from fiction."

Even though I had continued to refuse to review all of the events of the past months in detail with Dr. Harrison, I was on good behavior. I even started to eat a little. My reward was my own private room on one of the less restricted wards and freedom from the continual observations of the male orderlies. My window overlooked a beautiful garden, beyond which I could see the water. It must be nearly June, I thought. I could feel some life returning. I played a few games of tennis and began a daily regime of swimming in the indoor pool. In the evenings, we would play bridge. I was learning how to silkscreen and how to use the kiln to bake ceramics.

The medication must be working. Harrison had told

me that in his opinion my diagnosis was a depression, with an acute panic reaction that had led to extensive disorganization. If he was right, then after a few weeks on medicine, freedom from the stresses and strains of life beyond the gates of Sea View, and not being stirred up again and again by exposure to ideas about the supernatural, I would be all right again. The nightmare of all these months would be over.

I had had no strange experiences for nearly three weeks now. I slept soundly at night and without dreams. My mind was clearing, and my biggest concerns had become the day-to-day details of being at Sea View.

It was Valeric's third visit. I'd been in the hospital for two and a half weeks. She was visibly happy with my progress. We walked down to the beach and sat on the rocks, watching the gulls swoop down over schools of fish and hearing the gentle lap of the small waves on the shore.

"Maybe a different kind of life, Fred," Valerie suggested. "Maybe we should leave New York. You could have a smaller practice. I can write almost anywhere. Somewhere warm. Carmel, perhaps, or the Carolinas. I've always wanted a simple house, modern, with a pool, so you can roll right out of bed in the morning and take a dip."

"Sounds marvelous. You're probably right. Too many patients. Too many committees. Too much pressure. I thought I had it all well in hand."

"You did, darling. For years. But you weren't forty-five. Not that that's old! But being a psychiatrist means being under a lot of stress, and maybe you have to find a different kind of life-style now."

A large gray gull had landed and stood no more than two feet from us, studying Valerie carefully. In the distance, we could see a dozen red sails racing.

"I'll give it some thought."

"Mort sends his regards."

"I thought he was going to come up and see me."

"Next week. He also sends his apologies."

"For what?"

"For not insisting you get back into treatment sooner, and"—she laughed—"for being too much of an analyst to think of giving you antidepressants earlier."

"Well, we all learn. Stein's an honest man."

I had been gazing out across the water. I turned my head to look directly at Val. "You look beautiful," I said.

"I feel beautiful," Val replied. "Because I love you. And now I'm sure everything is going to be fine."

I drove with Valerie to the main gate. As I stood there watching her drive on, waving to her, and saw the white Volvo turn a distant corner out of sight, I had the terrible feeling that I might never see her again.

~ 21 ~

IT WAS THE FIRST LIQUORLESS-PUNCH-AND-DANCE NIGHT OF the month of June at the Plantation. All the patients who could hobble or think clearly enough to find their way to the auditorium were determined to come. The recreation budget permitted a three-piece band, which devoted itself to playing tunes from the sixties, especially the ones the Beatles had made popular. One song in particular, though not by the Beatles—"We've got to get out of this place, if it's the last thing we ever do"—struck a chord with nearly everyone there, and as the trio played it, the whole group sang along with as much passion as it could muster.

The orderly who had been assigned to watch me during my first days at Sea View approached me. "Well, I guess you'll be going home pretty soon," he said.

"I expect to."

"Your experience here should help you be a better doctor."

"Probably."

"Well, my hat's off to you. After the first week or so, you certainly dug in and took part in everything, just

209

like the other patients. That took guts."

"Not really. It's a no-choice situation. If I hadn't, I suppose I'd only be here longer. Besides, once I felt better, even a little better, I wanted to get well."

"Anyway—it's been a pleasure." He shook my hand.

I danced a couple of rounds, once with an elderly woman who, except for her dejection, reminded me of Margaret, and once with a teenage girl hardly older than Lisa, whom I knew to be extremely shy and terrified in any kind of social situation.

I decided to retire early. As I lay in my bed, reading an old Evelyn Waugh satire called *Put Out More Flags,* I could hear the band playing on, shifting now to music of the thirties. My eyes began to close. I barely noted it was about ten thirty, turned off the light, and fell asleep.

I was awakened by the sound of footsteps in the corridor just outside my room. I sat bolt upright in bed as my door was flung open. Two men were standing there, wearing black raincoats, silhouetted against the dim light.

"Pleiert. Now. Come," said one of them, beckoning with a wave of his arm. "Now." His voice was insistent.

I was still half asleep. "What is this?" I muttered.

"The way is clear. But you must come now. There isn't much time," said the other.

I stood up, bewildered, heart racing, breathing heavily, and stumbled toward the doorway. As I did so, the two figures seemed to move quickly down the corridor, around the corner, and out of sight. The hallway was now empty. I listened. The music from the party had stopped. I felt weak and leaned against the doorframe, my hand on the wall, only to pull it away again suddenly. The plaster was damp, and I felt it crumble in my hand.

I went back in my room long enough to put on

my dungarees and shirt. Then I began to walk, slowly, carefully, along the hall. At one point, I stopped and reached out to feel the wall again. My hand passed easily through the plaster, which had completely lost its solidity.

Where the hell is the charge nurse, I wondered. What's happening? Am I hallucinating again?

In the distance, I could hear the music once more. No, it wasn't music. It was the sound of voices, chanting, some kind of religious choir, singing a Kyrie. I tried to look out the windows, but a thick fog had come up and I could see nothing. The distant voices grew louder. A few feet ahead of me I saw a sign that read EXIT. The door beneath it was open. I stepped through.

I was outside in a courtyard. The night was cold. A fog had come up from the Sound. I could see the silhouette of the large main hospital building looming up in the distance. Light was coming from the auditorium section, struggling to penetrate the mist. I ran toward it through the damp grass. Looking in the windows, I could see the patients dancing, moving about like marionettes in slow motion, but I could not hear the music.

I walked quickly to the auditorium door. It was locked. Back at the windows I began to pound, again and again, with closed fists, calling out the names of a nurse and orderly who were standing right in front of the windows. They did not turn around. Everyone went on dancing, talking, laughing, in a pattern of jerking movement that became increasingly grotesque as I watched. But still no one heard me.

The nurse, who was no more than four feet away from me, turned toward the window and looked directly out, right at me. I pressed my face against the pane and banged hard with my hands. I was peering practically straight into her eyes, but she turned away again to watch the dancers.

My God, I thought, she doesn't see or hear me.

Suddenly I heard the sound of footsteps along the stone path that led to the building. I turned quickly around and saw figures moving toward me. It was hard to make them out in the darkness. Maybe a couple of people leaving the dance.

"Over here," I shouted, without thinking.

Now I could see them in the light cast from the windows. There were a dozen or more, dressed in black, moving stealthily toward me. As one of them entered an area of light cast from the auditorium window, I saw what looked like an antiquated rifle in his hand.

"Halt!" he called.

I ran to the door of the building and tried to open it again. It was locked.

"Halt," another shouted.

They moved closer. Now they were only about twenty feet away from me. One of them raised his gun, pointed it in my direction, and held it steadily.

"*Qu' est-ce que vous faites ici?*" a voice asked harshly.

"*Allons!*" another said. "*Nous voulons vous poser des questions.*"

They were shouting in French. I didn't comprehend all the words, but the meaning seemed evident.

"What am I doing? This is a hospital!" I stammered.

"Herr Doktor! Pleiert! Halt!" another voice shouted disagreeably.

I took one quick look toward the lighted windows and could still see the patients dancing. I looked back again at the man with the musket. This must be an apparition,

I thought. It can't be real! In a minute I'll wake up and find myself back in my room.

A thick ribbon of fog suddenly drifted between us. I began to run. I heard two sharp cracks and a loud voice telling me to stop. But I kept running, across the field, toward the water. At one point I tripped over a pile of wood. As I fell, I scraped my right knee. I looked quickly behind me and could see a dozen or more torches, the light diffused by the thickening fog, but clearly moving up in a closing circle toward my position. I stood up. My right knee ached and stung. I force myself to move on, limping slightly, walking quickly, sometimes running as much as my shortness of breath would allow toward the dock somewhere ahead.

I could feel the ground change under my feet. Grass gave way to sand and stones. I could hear the water gently washing up on the beach. The ring of torches moved steadily toward me. I could hear the voices, shouting incomprehensibly, growing louder and louder.

I heard several bursts of gunfire, and there was a sharp sting on the right side of my head. I reached up and felt the warm wetness of blood. I tore off my shoes, stripped down to my underwear, raced into the water, and began to swim. At first the water was lukewarm, but as I swam on, I could feel it growing colder and colder. If only I can hold on longer, I can get to him.

By now the water was bitter cold. I struggled to keep going, but I could feel an enormous sense of exhaustion spreading throughout my body. Suddenly, I could hardly breathe. A powerful, crushing pain seized me, not really a pain but more as though someone had stuck his fist inside my chest and was squeezing my lungs and heart.

I turned to look back to shore. The torches were strung out along the beach and, in the light they cast on the water, heads were bobbing up and down, arms reaching out, splashing as they tried to make headway through the icy ripples. The figures on shore were methodically firing at them.

The pain was growing more severe. I could hardly raise my arm to reach out in front of me. My body, heavy and aching, sank below the surface for a few seconds. I made one weak effort to pull my head up again, but my strength was all but gone. I began to sink, practically lifeless, down, under the water into the darkness below.

~ 22 ~

SO THIS IS WHAT DEATH IS LIKE, OR DYING, AT ANY RATE. The pain is gone. I am not breathing, but I am not afraid. Floating, weightless, under the surface of the water, in ultimate darkness. The lack of sensation is almost pleasurable. Utter silence.

Images. As if I were watching a silent film which appears, disappears, then appears again, without color.

Frederic at three. My mother walks across the room, bends over, and kisses me on the top of my head. Her hand on my cheek is warm.

Now I am standing on the shore, looking out across the water, and I see myself, struggling, arms thrashing in the small waves, trying to stay afloat, sinking, emerging again, shouting without sound. I watch calmly, curiously, saddened by my visible agony.

There are two houses. I have found the first, but it is not right. I must find the other house and the room in it overlooking the river. There is something I must do.

Eleven. Standing on the railway platform, saying good-bye to my father in his major's uniform. I can see the engine's steam and feel the grip of his hand on my

215

arm and the beginning tears in his eyes. Don't cry, Father. I cried when you died, but it was pointless to cry. See. I have died too. I am here.

There is still something I must do.

Don't cry, Valerie. I love you. It is Christmas and the children are small and we are decorating the tree and when they have gone to bed Valerie and I will spread the presents out.

Caroline. How lovely you look. Has the anguish left?

Now the images are gone. There is only darkness. Time is arrested. Only my consciousness remains in space that has collapsed.

Without before or after it is impossible to know when the voices started. Valerie speaking my name, softly. A strange voice, low-pitched, hollow, reaching through the darkness, calling me.

Oh, God. The terrible pain has come back. I cannot breathe. Please. Let me die. The water is so cold. With one great effort, I push my legs down and reach up with my outstretched arms and thrust my head above the water's surface to inhale the cold night air.

I can see the shoreline a few hundred feet away, too far to swim. But I must swim if I am to live. I want to live. Yes.

Suddenly I see a single light, moving toward me across the water, slowly, surely, unmistakably toward me, growing larger and larger. It must be a small boat.

"Can you hear me?" It is the voice of a man.

"Frederic. Can you hear me?"

The light is shining full on me now. There. There is the boat. I reach out to grip his hand.

"Can you hear me?"

"Yes. I hear you."

~23~

IN RECONSTRUCTING THE FOLLOWING ACCOUNT OF WHAT took place at Sea View during the weeks of which I have no memory, I owe the basic facts to Mort Stein, Adam Rheinhart, and Valerie. To fill in, I have used my own deductions, professional and otherwise. This is why I am telling it almost as if it had happened to someone else.

Harrison made the following notation in his records. "The night of June 3, Dr. Pleier left the dance early and went back to his room. When the night nurse made her rounds at eleven o'clock, she found him asleep. An hour later, at midnight, she reported that he was gone from his room; assuming that he had been restless and had taken a walk or perhaps had gone to the bathroom, she made a note of his absence in the chart but did not make any effort to locate him then. At one o'clock, she reported, he was again asleep in his bed.

"The next morning, however, he did not get up for breakfast, and when she tried to rouse him, he was totally unresponsive. She called the resident on duty. It was then seven in the morning. He, too, could not make

Pleier respond, but on a cursory neurological examination, he could find no signs of coma. The patient's reflexes were active, but when the resident attempted to get a reaction by first gently, and then firmly, stabbing a pin in his skin, he could not do so. He promptly called me. I arrived about fifteen minutes later and, after a few preliminary checks, lifted Pleier's arm upward. I found that wherever I positioned it, it remained without falling back to the bed again. (Catatonia?) The patient was transferred to a more restricted unit, and a neurologist called for a more thorough evaluation."

Within hours, Harrison broke the news of Frederic's relapse to a shocked Valerie, reassuring her that everything that could be done would be done and admitting that not only was the sudden appearance of a catatonia-like condition unexpected, it was totally out of keeping with the diagnosis and progress.

Valerie insisted that Mort Stein be called in as a consultant. He went to Sea View Monday morning. His note in the chart was brief. "Spent several hours trying to talk with patient to no avail. Have reviewed the results of various tests as completed. After discussion of case with Harrison and others, no consensus as to diagnosis. With considerable effort, the nurses can sit the patient up, guide him to a chair, encourage him to drink some orange juice and liquid protein supplement. But most of the time Pleier simply sits, eyes open, neither talking nor responding, as if unaware of others. Will follow."

It was on Margaret Gregory's insistence that Valerie finally agreed to call Adam Rheinhart. Rheinhart had, in fact, phoned Valerie a number of times during the hospitalization at Sea View, but she had requested that he stay out of the case. As far as she was concerned, Rheinhart's dabbling had only complicated whatever emotional difficulties might have been at work. But as nearly three weeks passed and she could see no signs of recovery, frightened by the inability of any of the doctors to explain Frederic's condition adequately, and prodded by Margaret, she asked Rheinhart to make an examination himself and confer with them. It was an act of desperation.

Harrison, of course, was not happy about the idea of such a consultation. Mort Stein, on the other hand, said it was best to keep an open mind.

The morning of June 26, twenty-two days after the onset of what Harrison still considered to be a catatonic state, he, Mort Stein, Rheinhart, and Valerie met together in his office at Sea View to review the situation and formulate plans for further care.

Harrison sat behind his large mahogany desk. His Phi Beta Kappa key hung from a gold chain strung across his vest. Mort Stein slumped in an easy chair, hands clasped, pensive. Valerie, who only a few weeks before had felt that everything was going to be all right, looked pale and thin. Hardly sleeping or eating, she had lost several pounds, and her eyes were dark from fatigue. She sat in a straight chair in front of Harrison's desk. A few feet to her left, Rheinhart sprawled on a leather sofa, arms crossed, legs stretched out in front of him, his expression solemn, as he listened to Harrison review what had been done.

"I don't have to tell you," Harrison went on, "that Dr. Pleier's condition is quite unusual. No history of schizophrenia, so we would not expect this sort of catatonic state. We've been operating on the assumption that he was suffering—and probably still is—with some kind of affective disorder." He paused to look at Valerie. "Depression, that is," he said. "And, as rarely happens, with the formation of delusions and hallucinations."

"Quite rare," Rheinhart commented.

"Rare"—Harrison's tone was defensive—"but not impossible."

"You say his early response to the antidepressants was good," Mort commented.

"Excellent," said Harrison. "You saw him during that time, and so did you, Mrs. Pleier, and he was fine."

Valerie trembled noticeably. "The day I came to visit the last time, I thought he was much better," she said.

Harrison continued, "Naturally we've done everything to rule out some physical disease. Blood and urine tests were negative. The CAT scan was also negative, ruling out a brain tumor or cerebrovascular accident." He again translated for Valerie. "There's no evidence of brain damage or a tumor, Mrs. Pleier. Two neurologists have reviewed the findings and examined him and they agree."

"An encephalitis of some kind?" asked Mort.

"No evidence."

"What did the EEG tracings show?" Rheinhart asked.

Harrison hesitated. "Well, I don't know what to make of them, frankly. In fact, I'd like you to look at them."

He pulled a stack of paper from a manila folder and opened it up. He handed it to Stein, saying, "Can you read it?"

"Enough to see that there were some distinct peculiarities in it," Stein replied. "What does the consultant's report say about it?" He handed it to Rheinhart, who began to examine it more closely.

"According to Dr. Malloy—he's from Yale—it is an

unusual pattern. His report is two pages long, but summing it up, Dr. Pleier's brain-wave pattern strongly resembles that of someone who is asleep, with the exception that instead of half the tracing consisting of a quiet pattern, it is almost ninety percent turbulent, typical of the dream phase of sleep associated with rapid eye movements. We've done a complete polysomnography examination, checking brain waves, eye movements, and the tension in the muscles, and there is no question about it. Pleier has a sleep record, even though he is obviously awake most of the time, and it is abnormally dominated by REM periods."

"Might that indicate that, even though he is apparently awake, he is in some kind of semiconscious condition, perhaps actively hallucinating?" Stein asked.

"It could indicate anything," Harrison stated bluntly. "This is certainly not the record of a catatonic patient. Nor is the finding typical of any known disturbance of consciousness or of the sleepwalking cycle."

"In other words," Rheinhart said quietly, "you don't know what it means."

"Exactly. But it is the only finding that is in any way unusual. Otherwise, I think we're faced with a patient who is in a state of severe withdrawal. Depression still seems to be the main feature of his condition, and our treatment plan should be guided largely by our clinical observations."

Mort Stein leaned forward. "You mean, you suggest we ignore this abnormality and guide ourselves entirely by what we have in Fred's history and progress in the hospital?"

"What else can we do?" Harrison replied.

"Based on that viewpoint, what do you have in mind, Dr. Harrison?'" Rheinhart asked.

Harrison was silent for a moment, anticipating a controversial response to his next words. "We've tried Dr. Pleier on the antidepressants and we've also added a major tranquilizer of the phenothiazine group, without success," he began.

"What about the possibility that we're dealing with an adverse reaction to the drugs?" Stein asked.

"Very unlikely. Besides, we stopped all medication a week ago and there's no change, one way or the other."

"Well, then?" Valerie broke in. "What do you want to do?"

"There is one treatment approach which works in depression and has been useful in catatonic states as well . . ." Harrison went on.

Mort Stein crushed out his cigarette in the ashtray he held on his lap, and as he did so, he said abruptly, "Come, now, Harrison, stop beating around the bush. We all know what you're driving at."

"I think we should give Pleier a course of electric shock," Harrison said.

Valerie was the only one in the room who could not have predicted Harrison's suggestion. She stiffened. But before she could say anything, Rheinhart stood up. "In the face of this brain-wave finding, you'd go ahead and give shock!"

"The brain-wave pattern tells us nothing, Dr. Rheinhart," Harrison replied adamantly.

"It tells us that we can't be sure what we're dealing with, and that's a lot," Rheinhart insisted.

"Come now, please," Mort Stein said, drawing on his years of talent for calming people down. "Sit down, Rheinhart."

"Sit down? You people are trying to decide what

to do for Frederic Pleier when you haven't the foggiest notion of what's wrong with him!"

"I suppose you have some other theory?" Harrison said with equal hostility.

"Take it easy," Mort Stein repeated. Then, turning toward Valerie, he said, "I'm sorry, Val. I know this must be confusing for you."

She had begun to cry. "Couldn't you have had your discussions without me and then tell me your conclusions?" she said, half in anger, half sadly.

"You had to be here, Mrs. Pleier," said Harrison kindly, regaining his composure. "Your husband is in no condition to make a judgment about his treatment, and therefore we can do nothing now on his behalf without your approval. I think it is important for you to understand as much as possible what is involved, including the fact that we cannot be entirely sure about it."

"But shock treatments?" Valerie asked. "How could you consider giving Fred shock treatments?"

"Valerie," said Mort. "Valerie. That's only a suggestion. And it may be the right one. You know that I'm a psychotherapist. I haven't given anyone electric shock since my days at Hopkins. I really don't like the idea of shock treatments. But I've seen some patients helped dramatically by them who could not be helped with any other method of treatment. So we mustn't rule it out prematurely. They're not so risky as many people have been led to believe. The memory problems pretty well clear up in a few weeks. But I think it's too soon to consider this option now."

"You have something else to offer, Dr. Stein?" Harrison asked. His tone was slightly facetious.

"Waiting."

"Waiting!" Harrison repeated impatiently.

"It seems to me that the chances of Dr. Pleier's coming out of this on his own may be excellent . . . provided we don't do anything to prevent him from doing so." Mort stood up, walked to the bookcases that lined the far end of the room, turned, and continued thoughtfully, "It seems to me that our biggest risk is making Fred worse. With the right kind of nursing support, keeping up his nutritional status, trying to reach him—I'd be willing to come up to see him a couple of times a week—I think we can ease him out of whatever he's in over a period of time."

He had touched a sensitive nerve in Harrison.

"Do nothing, in other words!" he exploded. "That's a typical analytic approach! Let Pleier sit there, dumbly, staring into space, for the next six months or maybe years, hoping that a few soothing words or a right interpretation will jolt him out of his stupor!"

"For Christ's sake, will you stop it!" Valerie shouted, banging her hands on the arms of her chair, then gripping them tightly. "Will you stop talking about Fred as though he were some kind of thing!"

Rheinhart's deep voice cut through her protest.

"It's my turn, gentlemen, to tell you what I think should be done for Dr. Pleier . . . and Valerie, I want you to listen to me, closely. The decision is in your hands, Valerie, and if you make the wrong choice, you may lose Fred—forever."

"You are only here, Dr. Rheinhart, because Mrs. Pleier asked me to invite you," Harrison stated. "I don't know why she did, but that's her business. And I'm willing to listen to anything you may have to offer as a psychiatrist. But that's all."

"That's not all, Dr. Harrison. However I came to

be here, I am here. And you will hear me out."

Rheinhart stood up, opened his briefcase, and took out a tape recorder. He attached a cord and plugged it into a wall socket. He placed the recorder on the desk.

"Before I play this for you, I want to explain something. It's my opinion that Frederic Pleier is suffering with a condition far more complicated than your traditional forms of mental disorder, a condition which, when we understand more about it, may seem no less mysterious to us than the influence of childhood on adult behavior"— he paused to look at Stein—"or the relationship between brain metabolism and schizophrenia." He looked directly at Harrison.

"I said I would welcome your psychiatric opinion, Rheinhart," said Harrison, "but I'm not interested in sitting here and having you expound on your theories of the supernatural. I know all about them from television," he added caustically.

Rheinhart went on as if he had not heard him. "There is growing evidence of life beyond physical death. That's hardly news," he said. "It's been the cornerstone of human thinking and religion since the beginning of time. Only in our current age of so-called rationality have we felt the need to dismiss the possibility of forces we cannot see and immediately control."

It was obvious he was going to have his say.

"I don't know whether reincarnation is a reality or not, and, if it is, we still know little of the processes involved. There is some evidence, impressive but not conclusive. I won't go into it now. But I want to inform you of the work that Willy Gutheim, in Germany, has been doing, because I think it may be relevant to what Dr. Pleier is suffering."

Valerie stared directly at Rheinhart.

"That's the person you sent Fred to meet in Germany," she said. Her tone was somewhat accusatory. "He sounds mad."

"Willy Gutheim is anything but mad, let me assure you. And we cannot ignore the implications of his thinking, at least not so far as Frederic is concerned. Hear me out. If Gutheim is wrong, we have nothing to lose. If he is right, we have everything to lose . . . if we ignore it."

"Come to the point," Harrison said curtly.

"The point is that Frederic Pleier may be in danger of losing his present existence because of some factor that is disrupting the fusion of his spirit—if we may call it that—into his present form or identity. Some inexplicable force may be tearing him out of his present life and pressing him to return to a previous one."

"Oh, for God's sake," Harrison exclaimed.

"Imaginative, to be sure," said Mort Stein.

"Dangerous is the word I would use to describe Pleier's condition," Rheinhart emphasized. His voice was stern and intimidating. "What we do not know," he went on, "is why this may be going on in Pleier. That's a matter of speculation. Gutheim made an effort to expose him to places and things that might have given us such a clue, but on the basis of that try we still have little to go on. The coincidence that the spirit of Fridericus Pleiert, someone who lived in the seventeenth century and perhaps even before that, has returned, by accident or on purpose, in the form of Frederic Pleier—the same name, perhaps even the same bloodline, and curiously with very similar professional and personal life patterns—may be part of it. We don't know. Maybe the fusion is safer if there is not so specific a similarity between the new person and the former one."

"You mean, if old Fridericus had come back as a salesman, it would have been a more secure reincarnation?" Mort Stein's curiosity, wide ranging as it was, had been touched, though his basic disbelief in Rheinhart's speculations was apparent.

Rheinhart ignored this. "More important, I believe, than the circumstances of Pleier's present life are those of his former one. Gutheim and I both suspect that the explanation for the inadequate fusion lies not so much in Frederic's present life but in the specific circumstances of his death in his former one. For some reason, the spirit, as I have called it, or the soul, if you wish to use that word, may be torn between its present adaptation and a need—a compelling need—to return to the past life to do something, to finish something, whatever."

"Nonsense," Harrison muttered.

"Perhaps," said Rheinhart.

"It is farfetched," said Mort Stein. "But in any case I don't see how it bears on what we do for Fred."

"What we do *not* do for Fred would be more to the point, Dr. Stein. If we follow either of the lines of treatment you two have suggested—shock treatments or simply waiting and an effort to gradually break through the patient's withdrawal—we would not be likely to do serious harm, provided he were mentally ill. But our real enemy in this case is time. If we waste any more time without actively trying to find out what may explain the paranormal possibilities of this problem, and try to modify the course, we may run out of time altogether."

"What do you mean, run out of time, Dr. Rheinhart?" Harrison asked.

"In your notes, Dr. Harrison, just before Dr. Pleier was discovered in his stuporous condition, there is a report of his having been missing from his room for about an hour, am I correct?"

"The nurse thought he might have gone to the bathroom or taken a walk."

"For an hour, in the middle of the night? I believe that for that period of time, the patient was not in the hospital at all. I believe he had completely disappeared as a person in time. I'm also convinced this is not the first time this has happened. If we do not do something, I believe that it will not be the last. The risk we run is that Frederic Pleier will vanish, permanently, irreversibly."

Totally unable to accept any such possibility, Harrison and Stein nonetheless sat silently, as if intimidated by Rheinhart's authoritative tone.

"I want you to hear something," Rheinhart stood up and, walking to the desk, pressed the PLAY button on the tape recorder. In a couple of seconds, the voice of a man with a slight German accent emerged from the speaker, as Rheinhart said softly, "That's Gutheim."

"I found Dr. Pleier in the Jewish cemetery in Worms at two thirty in the morning, fourth of May. He had left his room at the Dom Hotel around eight to go to dinner. When he had not returned by eleven, I grew concerned and went looking for him. The girl at the hotel reception desk informed me he had made a long-distance call to the United States. Afterward, on her suggestion, he had gone to a restaurant on the far side of the Dom Platz for dinner. I inquired of the manager, who recalled seeing Dr. Pleier and described him as behaving strangely. The doctor had peered into the restaurant for several minutes before entering and, although standing alone outside the window, acted as though he were carrying on a conversation with some other person, though there was no one in evidence. He read throughout dinner. In paying his check, he had inadvertently made an error in calculating his exchange rate, and when the cashier followed him out of the door to give him the several marks due, no more than a few seconds behind him, he had disappeared. There was no way he could have reached a corner or alley in the time that passed.

"Alarmed, I notified the police. An active search was made through the center of town. No sign of Dr. Pleier was evident. The cemetery had already been carefully checked by the police, who finally abandoned their general search, planning to renew it in the morning. On the verge of quitting myself, I came on him near the far wall of the cemetery. My conclusion is that, for a period of four or five hours, Dr Pleier was not present in our time, that he had, in fact, lapsed into a state of disintegration while taking on a former identity."

There was a pause on the tape, no more than a few seconds, then the voice resumed.

"Interview with Dr. Pleier, Dom Hotel, four A.M. Dr. Pleier is obviously in a state of considerable confusion, moving in and out of consciousness, at times incoherent."

A second voice was heard on the tape. Valerie was startled and exchanged looks with Mort. The voice was uneven, faint, but unmistakably Fred's.

"Willy? Willy? What happened?"

"You are all right now, Friedrich. You will be fine now."

(Pause.)

"Tell me, Friedrich. What do you remember?"

"There were these two men . . . dinner . . . I don't know . . . what time is it, Willy . . .?"

"A little past four."

(Pause.)

Suddenly a third voice was heard on the tape, deeper than Frederic's, speaking slowly in German.

"I'll read a translation as we go along," Rheinhart whispered.

"I have left them with Jacob," said the voice.

"Who is Jacob?" It was Willy again, also speaking German.

"Anna Katherine. I must go back to her."

"Where is Anna Katherine?"

"In the tunnel . . . no . . . we have left the tunnel . . . we are with Jacob . . . at the synagogue . . . someone is to meet me here . . . I must go . . . the Frenchman is dead . . ."

"What tunnel? What Frenchman?" Willy was gently prodding.

"In the cathedral crypt . . . the French soldiers came . . . they raped . . . we killed one of them . . . escaped through the tunnel . . ."

"Escaped? Escaped to where?"

There was a long pause. Then a cry of anguish. "They have cut off their heads and put them on spikes above the gates. The city is burning, everywhere . . . we cannot flee . . . snow . . . too cold . . ."

Silence. The sound of heavy breathing. Then, "Jacob. Jacob will help us. He promised. When I pleaded for him and his people, two years ago, to keep them from being expelled from the city, and the townspeople listened to me and relented, he promised. The soldiers will keep the Jews alive, for ransom. He will protect us. Jacob promised and Jacob's word is law."

Again, a seemingly endless pause.

"Friedrich?" Willy urged softly. "What is happening? Friedrich?"

"Anna Katherine and the children . . . safe now with Jacob. He had a plan . . . I am to go to the cemetery, hide there, wait for dark . . . must go alone . . . Basel . . ."

Ever so faintly, it sounded like a man sobbing.

Willy's voice again. "Friedrich?"

Then, in English: "Willy? Is that you?" It was Fred. "What's happening, Willy?"

Rheinhart pushed the OFF button.

"There's no point in your listening to the entire tape now. It runs on for nearly two hours, sometimes rambling, incoherent, sometimes frighteningly clear. I wanted you to hear enough to realize that Dr. Pleier did vanish in Worms and to listen to that other voice."

"Belonging to?" Harrison asked.

"Fridericus," Rheinhart said firmly.

"Ridiculous," Harrison said. "It's some kind of trick."

"I've known Adam for years. It's no kind of chicanery," said Mort Stein. "Unless," he added, "this Willy is trying to put something over on you, Adam."

"I trust him without reservation," said Rheinhart.

"Has Pleier heard this tape?" Harrison asked, accusingly.

"No. Willy was afraid to let him, lest it trigger a severe reversion."

Valerie sat there, her head in her hands, sobbing. She looked up. "What are you trying to say?" she asked. "That that other voice on the tape is someone out of the past?"

"Yes—in Frederic's body," Rheinhart said gently. "Aside from the quality of the voice, Frederic told me he doesn't speak German. I remember assuring him that Willy would make an excellent interpreter."

Valerie was frowning. "It seems to me that he once mentioned having had a German nurse as a very small child. Is it possible he could have learned some German from her?"

"He did have a German nurse," Mort Stein said. "He mentioned her in his analysis. It's unlikely, but it is possible, under extreme stress, to dredge up very early language imprints and use them. Freud reported a case like that."

"We'll have to discount the German, then," Adam Rheinhart said, "at least for the present. Although the amount of it on the tape is certainly noteworthy. As for the name Anna Katherine, I believe that name appears as the name of Fridericus's wife on some biographical material Fred had obtained from Germany before he went. That leaves us, for this type of evidence, only the talk of Jacob, who was the leader of the Jewish community in Worms at that time, and the mention of the tunnel. Apparently, neither of these details was previously known to Frederic Pleier."

"To take Jacob first," Mort said, "surely Fred could have read about him somewhere."

"It's most unlikely that he would be familiar with such a little-known fact as the name of that particular Jew, who achieved no particular prominence in history."

"How do we know it's a fact at all?" Harrison said. "Maybe he made it up."

"I'm afraid not," Adam said. "Gutheim sent me documents showing that Jacob was indeed head of that community in 1631, records I do not believe Frederic could have had any prior access to. As for the tunnel . . ."

"If there is a tunnel," said Harrison skeptically.

"There isn't now," Rheinhart answered. "But there was one, then. It was destroyed in the bombings during the last war. It is not referred to in any of the guidebooks on Worms. But Willy was able to verify that it did exist in the seventeenth century. A history professor he knew in Worms helped him find a reference to it in an obscure volume. They then located it on an old map. This was not accomplished until Fred was, in fact, already at Sea View. I have photocopies of both documents."

Harrison started to say something, but Rheinhart overrode him. "In any event, I must emphasize to all of you that these details are only incidental to the real meaning of this tape. It is a record of the very sort of thing that Frederic Pleier is probably experiencing right now—sitting there like a vegetable while his abnormally dominant REM periods show God knows what sort of turbulence he is going through in some other . . . some other reality."

Everyone was silent for a moment.

Mort Stein was the first to speak. "Well, Adam. You've certainly put on an impressive presentation, as you always do." He had returned to his chair and now reached his hand out to rest it, comfortingly, on top of Valerie's. "On the basis of your own thinking, what do you propose?"

"I'd like a spend a few days here with Frederic. I want to see if, using hypnosis, I can reach him and find out what is going on."

"You can't hypnotize a catatonic patient, Adam," said Mort. "You know that."

"I've made it quite clear that I don't think Frederic is catatonic—or depressed either."

"And if we permit this and if you fail, Rheinhart, then what?" asked Harrison sternly.

"Then you and Mort Stein can go back to arguing about shock treatments."

"Well, I for one am opposed to it," Harrison said, leaning back in his desk chair, hands resting on the top of the blotter. "I think it's too risky."

"I'm afraid I too think there's a risk associated with it, Adam," said Mort Stein. "If we are dealing with a delusional system that incorporates ideas of reincarnation, then I think what you are suggesting could reinforce Frederic's pathology, perhaps irreversibly. You know, we like to think we can help everyone, and we have come a long way, but the fact is that there are still plenty of patients in hospitals . . ." He tightened his hold on Valerie's hand. "I'm sorry, my dear, but I must say it—who remain disorganized and never recover. I think the risk is too great."

Rheinhart looked directly at Valerie. "I'm sorry too, Valerie. But you have to help us make the choice. I cannot tell you how critical I feel it is for you to let me try."

Valerie said nothing as she moved her hand from underneath Mort's and, resting it on top of his, squeezed it tightly. Then she said slowly, "How can I know what is best? It's not fair to ask me. I hardly know you, Dr. Harrison. And as for you, Dr. Rheinhart, I don't know whether to regard you as a visionary or a menace. I wouldn't have asked you to come here if I didn't feel so helpless"—she paused a moment—"and if I didn't think that Frederic wanted you to help him."

She looked at Mort. "Mort. Please. What should I do?"

"You know what I think, Valerie."

Valerie rose, walked across the room to the wide

window, and looked out on the hospital lawn. She noticed a couple of young women patients, playing tennis, and a nurse guiding several elderly patients to the benches near the dock, where they could sit quietly in the sun until lunchtime. A man in his mid-thirties was being escorted by two male orderlies toward the large red-brick building where she knew the disturbed unit was located. The man was tremulous, shaking as he walked, and on his face was an expression of vacant resignation.

She walked to the front of Harrison's desk and put her hand on Rheinhart's tape recorder. She pushed the PLAY button. A thick, guttural voice spoke hoarsely a few words she did not understand, in German. Then, she heard Fred's voice, bewildered, asking Willy, "What's happening, Willy?"

She pushed the OFF button.

"If you do what you want to do, Dr. Rheinhart," she said, almost in a whisper, "you won't hurt him, will you?"

"No more than I have to, Valerie."

She sighed.

"Do what you have to do, Dr. Rheinhart," she said. "It would have been Fred's choice. It is mine."

~24~

WILLY GUTHEIM AGREED TO FLY TO THE STATES AS SOON AS
he received Rheinhart's phone call. Adam Rheinhart
wanted him there during the hypnosis. Also with Valerie's
permission, Rheinhart arranged to video-tape the sessions.

Harrison had at first asked Valerie to arrange for
Rheinhart to use another hospital for the hypnotic experiment—he didn't want the responsibility, but Mort Stein
convinced him otherwise. So, in the end, he arranged for
a room in the main office building where Rheinhart could
carry out the work. In one wall of the room there was a
two-way mirror window through which he and Stein could
observe what was happening. If he felt things were getting
out of hand, Harrison made it clear, he would instantly
signal a halt.

Rheinhart planned on a half a dozen hypnotic sessions, over a period of three days, each lasting about two
hours. He had reluctantly promised that if he could not
succeed in that length of time and with that many sessions,
he would discontinue all such efforts with Pleier.

The room itself was practically bare. There were
no pictures on the walls, only the large, rectangular, built-

in mirror, on the window side of which Harrison and Stein sat watching. There was a large comfortable leather chair for Pleier with soft cushions and a footstool. Rheinhart sat next to it. He had set up a special light on a stand which blinked on and off as a circular, perforated disk moved steadily across the beam. Willy sat several feet farther back, behind the light. Otherwise, the room was entirely dark.

The first three sessions were complete failures; Rheinhart was endlessly patient, but unable to elicit any response whatever. By noon of the second day, Harrison was trying to persuade him to give up, but Rheinhart insisted on his three more sessions as promised.

That afternoon, Rheinhart dictated, for the videotape recording, "June twenty-ninth, two thirty P.M. Fourth attempt to hypnotize Dr. Pleier." Then he switched the room light off and the small lamp on, and began again the long process:

"Watch the light, Frederic. See the light, flickering on and off. Frederic. This is Adam Rheinhart. Can you hear me?"

Again and again he repeated the instructions, slowly, distinctly. He would stop every five minutes or so, rest, then begin again. He was now about twenty minutes into the session.

Suddenly, Pleier lifted one hand very slightly, then dropped it back on the chair arm. Mort Stein, watching, leaned forward.

"Can you hear me?" Rheinhart asked.

"Yes. I hear you." The voice was faint, barely a whisper.

"Frederic. This is Adam Rheinhart. Do you know who I am?"

"Yes."

"Watch the light, Frederic. Let your body relax. Do not be afraid." He repeated the phrases again several times. Then, "I am going to ask you some questions, Frederic, and I want you to answer them. Do you understand?"

"Yes."

"What is your name?"

"Frederic Pleier."

"How old are you?"

"Forty-five."

"Are you married?"

"Yes."

"What is the name of your wife?"

"Valerie."

"Do you have any children?"

"Yes."

"How many?"

"Two."

"What are their names?"

There was no answer. He restated the question. "Frederic. What are the names of your children?"

"Lisa . . . Jennifer."

"How old are they?"

Again, there was no answer. But before he could ask the query again, Frederic said, "I don't know."

"What kind of work do you do, Frederic?"

"I'm a doctor."

"What kind of doctor?"

"A doctor."

"What year is it?"

"Nineteen seventy-eight."

"Do you know where you are?"

"In a hospital."

"Do you know the name of the hospital?"

"Sea View."

"Why are you here, Frederic?"

"Because I've had a breakdown. Sick."

"What is wrong with you?"

"I don't know."

Before Rheinhart could proceed with another question, a deeper voice whispered hoarsely, *"Ich im sterben liege."*

Rheinhart stiffened, then motioned to Willy. "Translate," he said tersely.

"I am dying," Willy said softly.

Harrison had had installed a small signal light with which he or Stein could communicate with Rheinhart during the experiment. It flashed on, pale green. Rheinhart picked up the tiny earphone which sat on the table beside him and listened.

"Too risky, Rheinhart." It was Harrison. "If Pleier thinks he's dying, you might push him into a psychophysiological reaction that could kill him."

Rheinhart took a large pad and pencil, wrote his reply in large, emphatic capitals, and held it up for the viewers to see: CHANCE I HAVE TO TAKE!

He turned back to the patient. "What do you mean, Frederic? Why are you dying?"

"Drowning."

It was said in English, but Rheinhart and Willy could barely hear it.

"Frederic. I can't hear what you said. Please repeat your answer."

"Drowning."

Rheinhart appeared puzzled by the answer. "Are you in the water?"

"Swimming."

"Where are you swimming, Frederic?"

"In the river."

"Why are you swimming there?" Rheinhart asked.

"There is something I have to do."

"What do you have to do?"

"I don't know."

"How did you get there?"

"I don't know."

"What do you have to do, Frederic?"

There was no response. Rheinhart continued his questions, returning in a few minutes to earlier ones—name, wife's name, names of children—but he was unable to get any more answers.

"That's enough for now, Frederic. Relax. Go to sleep. When you awaken, you will feel refreshed."

After the session was over, Harrison warned Rheinhart that if his opinion was disregarded once again, the whole experiment would be called off and he would insist that Valerie agree with his suggestion for shock treatments or transfer elsewhere.

"June thirtieth, nine thirty A.M. Fifth session."

Rheinhart was again able to make contact. The responses to his initial questions were made in a stronger voice than in the previous session. But when he was asked the names of his children, the first reply was, "I do not know."

Instead of repeating the question, Rheinhart said, "Why don't you know the names of your children?"

No response.

"Frederic." The tone was insistent. "Why don't you know the names of your children?" After a long silence

240

he asked, "Where are your children, Frederic? Where are they?"

"My children are dead."

"How did they die?"

"My daughters of the plague. My son . . ."

"Your son?" Reinhart prompted.

"Not dead."

"What is your son's name?"

"Matthius."

"What is his mother's name?"

"Anna Katherine."

Willy breathed in sharply as tears began to flow down Frederic Pleier's tortured face while he moved abruptly in the chair, trying to raise himself up as if against some powerful force.

"What is the matter, Frederic?"

"I must go. There is something I must do."

"Please. Sit back, quietly," Rheinhart said.

"Let me go. Let me go. I am dying. I must . . ."

The green warning signal went on. Rheinhart ignored it. "What do you have to do?"

There was a sigh of defeat; the body slumped back in the chair.

"What is your name?" Rheinhart asked, firmly.

No response.

"What is your name?" he repeated.

"Fridericus."

Harrison rose, left the viewing room, and opened the door to confront Rheinhart. Just as he was about to enter, Willy stood up, walked over to him, pushed him outside, and closed the door behind both of them.

Rheinhart continued. "What do you have to do?"

The eyes were closed. Respiration had stopped.

Rheinhart leaned forward to feel the pulse. He was unable to detect a beat. Opening the bathrobe, he placed his hand against the rib cage. Again, he could feel nothing.

"Breathe, Frederic. Breathe deeply and open your eyes," he ordered sternly.

Willy had reentered quietly. Harrison was racing down the hallway to get a resident and the nurse on the cardiac emergency unit, cursing Rheinhart as he ran.

"Breathe, Frederic," Rheinhart repeated. "Open your eyes and breathe."

"German," Willy whispered. "Let me speak to him in German." Then he said, "Friedrich. Open your eyes and breathe regularly." He repeated it again, slowly, steadily, and then a third time.

The first breath was deep, gasping, almost a groan. Rheinhart's palm on the chest detected a heartbeat, faint at first, but gradually gaining in strength. Willy continued to speak in German.

"What is wrong, Friedrich?"

The answer came in a deep, guttural voice—the same voice that Willy had heard and taped after he had found Frederic in the cemetery in Worms.

"Great pain . . . in chest . . . drowning."

"Where are you?"

"In the river."

"What river?" Willy asked.

No response.

"How did you get to the river, Friedrich?"

"Two men . . . helped me escape . . . current too strong . . . must reach Matthius. He will die. He is all I have left. The water is so cold. The pain is so great . . . I can hardly move my body through the water."

"What is happening to Matthius?"

"He is drowning."

With that, Frederich Pleier sat upright in the chair, gripped its arms tightly, and gave a cry so loud that both Gutheim and Rheinhart were startled. The door opened suddenly. Harrison strode into the room, followed by the resident and the nurse with the cardiopulmonary resuscitator.

"Stay back," Rheinhart ordered. "His heart and breathing are fine. Stay back or you will risk it all!"

In spite of his demand, the nurse moved forward, felt the pulse, quickly listened to the heart with a stethoscope, and nodded affirmatively to Harrison. Then she stepped back.

"Where is your son drowning, Friedrich?" Willy asked.

"Near the city . . ." The voice was almost indistinct now. "Rhine . . . fire everywhere . . . boat . . . soldiers . . . shooting at us . . ."

"Friedrich. What about the boat?"

"Capsized . . . Matthius there, right there, only a few arm lengths away from me. He cannot swim. I must reach him . . . but the pain is so great . . . I cannot breathe . . . I am sinking . . . dear God, let me reach him."

All the while, Mort Stein had sat behind the mirror window, totally engrossed in what was transpiring, bewildered, half disbelieving his own senses, half convinced he was witnessing the rare double-personality phenomenon, shaken by it all.

Rheinhart whispered something in Willy's ear.

"What is happening now, Friedrich?" Willy asked. No response.

"Your pain is less. You are breathing well. Your strength is returning. Swim, now, toward Matthius," Willy commanded.

"No, Willy, no," Rheinhart said severely in low

tones. "You must not direct him to do that! You cannot change an event! If the boy died, he must die. If Fridericus died, he must die."

Harrison, hearing Rheinhart's words, started to move forward. Rheinhart held up his hand in an adamant gesture. "Ask him a more general question," he advised Willy.

"What is happening, Friedrich?" Willy inquired.

"I cannot see Matthius. I cannot see him!" There was an unmistakable tone of despair.

"Tell him that he *must accept* the boy's death," whispered Rheinhart.

"Matthius is dead," Willy said, gently. "You must accept that. You cannot change it, Friedrich. He is dead."

For an instant, Frederic's face apparently flushed with agonizing rage. Then a scream of fury, then silence. The nurse rushed forward.

"No pulse, Doctor," she said and quickly beckoned the resident. He stripped away the bathrobe and pajama top, pressed his fist firmly on the chest, and began to massage the heart.

"Nothing," he said.

Together they attached the electrodes. He pushed the switch, once, twice.

"I'm picking up a beat," the nurse said, using the stethoscope. She listened for several minutes.

The resident checked her observation. "He'll be all right now, I think," he said, turning toward Harrison.

"Take him back to the emergency unit and watch him carefully," Harrison ordered.

When they had gone, Harrison pulled a handkerchief from his pocket and wiped his brow, glaring at Rheinhart and Gutheim, as Mort Stein joined them.

"You took one hell of a chance, Rheinhart," Harrison said furiously. "If he doesn't come through this, I'll have your license!"

"It was a chance we had to take," Rheinhart replied without hesitation.

"That remains to be seen, Adam," Mort Stein said. There was a note of sadness in his voice.

~25~

FREDERIC PLEIER REMAINED UNCONSCIOUS FOR THREE DAYS
following the final hypnosis session. Harrison had arranged
for him to be transferred back to a private room on an
open unit, under constant surveillance, once his cardiac
state had stabilized. Valerie, who was staying with Margaret
and Alfred, drove to Sea View every afternoon after lunch
and sat by his side quietly, trying to read an Agatha Christie
mystery. While she was there, the nurse assigned to moni-
tor the patient would leave, returning when Valerie was
ready to go off for dinner. She scarcely spoke with Adam
Rheinhart, Willy Gutheim, Dr. Harrison, or, for that matter, Mort Stein. Perhaps, she brooded, she should have
agreed to Harrison's suggestion of shock, or to Mort
Stein's idea of doing nothing but let him come out of it
on his own. If he dies, she kept repeating to herself, if
he dies, I will have been the one who had made the choice.

She was there when he first stirred and opened his
eyes. In a clear, strong voice, he said her name. The paper-
back fell to the floor as she stood up, leaned down, and
took him in her arms.

Harrison was called immediately. He carefully examined Frederic and then returned to his office, where he found Mort Stein waiting for him.

"It's incredible," Harrison said. "He looks and acts fine, as if nothing had ever happened."

"I'll go up and see him as soon as we're finished."

Harrison was clearly puzzled. "I don't understand it," he said.

"Frankly, neither do I," said Mort.

"He's a little confused about what's been going on, of course. No recollection of the hypnosis sessions. The last thing he recalls clearly is coming back to his room from the dance."

"Exactly a month ago!"

"And dreaming wildly," Harrison went on. "Being chased, swimming, nearly drowning."

"Then he does remember some of the material that came out under hypnosis."

"Bits and pieces. He thinks it was a nightmare."

"And what did you tell him?"

Harrison paused. "I told him he'd been out of contact for weeks, some kind of coma or hysterical stupor."

"Did you tell him about Rheinhart and the hypnosis?"

"Yes," he replied hesitantly. "I figured he'd find out about it anyway—from Rheinhart or his wife." Harrison began to draw geometric designs on a piece of scrap paper. "He wants to see the video tapes of the sessions."

"You don't have much choice but to let him, do you?" Mort replied.

"I'm afraid not. Besides, it'll be a test of just how real his improvement is."

"What's your diagnosis now?" Mort asked thoughtfully.

"I still stick to the idea of a depression. Never seen one quite like this, but there's always a first time."

"You don't buy Rheinhart's theories?"

"Are you serious? That lunatic!" Harrison thundered.

"Rheinhart thinks he can make a pretty convincing case. He believes he has plenty of evidence."

"Evidence!" Harrison said contemptuously. "You call that evidence! There's nothing on those tapes or in Dr. Pleier's history that can't be explained on the basis of what we know about psychiatric disturbances. In fact, since Pleier is a psychiatrist himself, I see no reason why he couldn't twist and bend his own symptoms . . . unconsciously, of course . . . to create a highly unusual syndrome. But a syndrome, nonetheless."

He looked directly at Mort Stein. "And just what do you think?"

"I don't know. Certainly I can't accept the idea of something supernatural going on. I have to agree with you. But as to what it is, I really don't know."

Stein stood up and walked slowly toward the door. Harrison called after him.

"One thing you can do. Pleier's pushing to leave tomorrow. I told him he'd have to wait at least a week, to be sure he's as well as he thinks he is. I don't trust it. Would you talk to him, persuade him to go along with that?"

"I'll try."

~26~

HARRISON'S CONCERN ABOUT THE TENUOUSNESS OF MY recovery proved to be unnecessary. Most patients, when they've been through a serious emotional illness, pick up the threads of their lives slowly, cautiously, while mending the way a broken limb mends. From the moment I opened my eyes and saw Valerie sitting there next to my bed, I felt a calmness and certainty different from anything I had ever known. I wanted to leave Sea View that day, but Mort Stein persuaded me to stay on another week, not so much because of Harrison's insistence as out of consideration for Valerie.

During that week Harrison ran the video tapes of the hypnosis sessions for me. I was fascinated, yet at the same time curiously detached. Although I could still vividly recall the experiences of the past year, the memories were now stripped of emotion, devoid of the anxiety and fear that the actual events had triggered, as if it had all happened to a stranger.

Before Willy Gutheim left Sea View to catch his plane back to Frankfurt, he came to say good-bye. Adam Rheinhart was with him. I told Willy that I could now understand why he hadn't played the tape for me in Worms and apologized for having momentarily distrusted him. When I used the word "paranoid" to describe my reaction and said it was only further evidence of my extreme disorientation at the time, he seemed somewhat annoyed.

"Friedrich," he said with frustration. "Your use of psychiatric terms makes it sound as if you believe you've had a nervous breakdown."

"It couldn't be anything else," I replied firmly.

"How can you say that? The facts speak for themselves!" He stared at me indignantly.

Rheinhart interceded gently. "Never mind, Willy. Frederic has his way of looking at things. We have ours. The trouble with knowing," he went on, "is that what we think we know usually keeps us from seeing what we could come to know if we were not so committed to our existing point of view."

"But don't you think it's important for Friedrich to understand?" Willy asked.

"What's important," Rheinhart said, turning to me, "is for Frederic Pleier to survive. How we interpret the facts is quite another matter."

After Rheinhart returned back to California, I considered going back into analysis for a while, but decided against it. That was all right with Mort Stein, since things seemed to be going well. I was working again, though not as many hours as before the breakdown. There were no more nightmares, no strange experiences, not even as much as a passing doubt about the reality of my day-to-day life.

In early November, I ran into Mort at the University Club. He had time for a quick drink.

"You do look marvelous, Fred. From everything I hear, life is really back to normal."

"Better than that."

He smiled. "Not too up, I hope."

"Nothing like that, Mort. Just that I haven't felt as put-together in my entire life."

"As long as a few things make you nervous or get you down from time to time, like the rest of us," he said.

I hesitated for a moment. "Actually, I'm beginning to try to sort things out in my mind. As you know, I've been convinced I had a nervous breakdown. But lately, certain things I don't know what to make of keep nagging at me. And there's no one to discuss them with."

"How about Val?"

"I can't. Or at least, I don't want to. She's happy now . . . wants to leave it all behind us. As far as she's concerned I'm myself again, and that's all she cares about."

"But that's not enough for you?"

"Most of the time it is. I can pretty well account for almost all the things that happened to me. But some of them cannot be explained in terms of a breakdown. I've tried to figure everything out . . . a process of elimination. For example, I found the Worms tunnel mentioned in an old guidebook to Germany, one my family had, predating the Second World War. I might have seen it there."

"You're certainly familiar with hypermnesia experiments that show people can recall ten times as much under the influence of hypnosis as they can in the waking state," Mort commented.

"Of course. And that might also account for my knowing Jacob's name—maybe some input I've forgotten. But what about the Matthew-Matthius coincidence?"

251

After a moment's pause, Mort asked, "What did happen to the Holbein boy?"

"They still haven't found him."

He sighed. "I have to admit that when I made that connection while I was watching the hypnosis sessions, it really startled me." He shrugged his shoulders. "Some things, I'm afraid, will remain a mystery."

"Perhaps. But that's hard to accept."

"Why don't you write it all down?" he suggested. "Maybe that will make it easier for you. Put it on paper as best you can remember. That way you'll be better able to take a more objective look at it. And frankly, I wouldn't mind seeing what you come up with myself."

I felt a slight reservation. "I'm a little nervous about that, Mort. Might stir things up again."

"I don't think so, Fred. Not this time. I'm the one who originally told you to leave it alone. But I feel quite comfortable with the idea now. Why don't you try it?"

Our reference to Matthew's disappearance triggered my realization that I had never told either Adam Rheinhart or Willy Gutheim anything about the Holbein case. I'd thought it irrelevant when I first went to Washington to see Adam, and later, in my panic and distrust, I had withheld the story from Willy. I felt they were entitled to know and decided to write them both.

I heard from Adam by return mail.

> My dear Frederic:
> I am so pleased to hear everything is going well with you. I agree with Mort. It would be a good idea for you to document your recollections of the past year. Naturally I would like to see your notes when you've finished them.
> As for Matthew Holbein, your information did

come as a bit of a surprise. I doubt that knowing it earlier would have made any difference in my own thinking at the time or in the advice I gave you. And it may still be nothing more than coincidence. I am increasingly convinced, however, of the validity of Gutheim's fusion theory, and it might well be that the boy was subject to such a problem. As to whether he could have been Fridericus's son, it seems plausible to me, although I doubt it would fit into your way of looking at things.

Perhaps Matthew Holbein will eventually turn up in any case.

My best to Valerie.

Adam

Rheinhart came to our home for dinner in February, during a visit to New York in the middle of the worst blizzard in years. He was on his way to a conference in Rome. We spoke of his work and ours, but no reference was made to what I had gone through, more for Val's sake than my own. It was obvious, in both our attitudes toward him, that she and I were deeply grateful to him and to Willy.

I heard from Willy once again. He sent me a manuscript for my approval, a paper based on my experience that he intended to submit to a scientific journal. In it, he included a discussion of the Matthew-Matthius connection, suggesting that one might have been the reincarnation of the other but leaving the question open for speculation. The names had been changed to protect everyone's privacy.

In his covering letter Willy told me that, as I had requested in a postscript when I wrote to inform him about Matthew Holbein, he had inquired whether there was an American Army base in or near Worms. There was. As far as I was concerned, that tied up one more loose end. Those two figures in the black raincoats must have been U.S. soldiers, no matter how my mind had distorted them.

Last month I received a letter from a search committee considering Ted Harrison for the chairmanship of the Department of Psychiatry at a major medical school. They wanted my opinion. I replied he would make a fine candidate. He was, after all, an excellent clinician.

Nearly a year has passed, now, since Sea View. There has been no recurrence of nightmares or any abnormal episodes, and Mort's suggestion that I recount the whole experience, although troublesome at times, has proved to be therapeutic. Of course, when you have been through what I went through, nothing can ever be quite the same again. But here, on the porch of our beach cottage in Rhode Island, while I wait for Valerie and the children to return so we can have a cookout, it all seems far away, like a dream I cannot recall with any clarity or even be sure I dreamed at all.

This fall, Lisa will be a sophomore in college. Jenny starts second grade. Valerie has grown to trust again. Intuitively she knows that I have somehow gained a completeness, a genuineness, and that she need never again fear its rupture.

Looking out across the moors toward the dune, I can dimly see the three of them coming back from the surf. Lisa is waving. Valerie walks hand in hand with Jenny, the aluminum beach chair gripped beneath her other arm.

As I finish this account, only the memory of Matthew persists as a lingering question in my mind, whispering a hint of immortality.

Demco, Inc. 38-293